THE
EASTER
BASKET
CASE

A
COLLABORATIVE
NOVELLA

The Easter Basket Case

Written by Mr. Cowgill's 2004 AP Literature Class

Photo credit: Jim Frost

To the crazy class of 2004
and to Mr. Geoff Cowgill

Forward

When Mr. Cowgill announced to us that the final project for our Advanced Placement Literature class would be to collectively write a novella, the reaction was mixed. Surprise was the overarching feeling. We had done plenty of creative projects in our four years at Argenta-Oreana High School, including writing fictional stories. But a novel? Just how long was a "novella" anyway? And... collaboratively?

i

The ground rules were simple: Six full pages, double spaced, Times New Roman 12. Each chapter would be graded on how well it met the requirements, maintaining and advancing the story, writing mechanics, and general effort and creativity. Worth 50 points, it was a significant chunk of our final grade.

In a way, it was scary. Free license to let your imagination roam! What would our creative writing say about us as individuals? And to rely on the person before you to set you up for success and the person after you to carry on with the story? Reading the book, you can see that play out. Chapters end with a cliff-hanger, or an obvious trap – the previous writer thinking mischievously to him- or herself, "How will the next writer get out of this?" Other chapters begin with a complete tangent from where the previous writer left off – the next writer changing pace. Some chapters attempt to nullify one chapter, dismissing it as a dream or delusion. And still more chapters to question the validity of that "dream". The way the authors interact with each other on the page is the most entertaining part of the book, you may find.

But with the Easter bunny as our protagonist – committing multiple murders of innocent people in very violent ways – it doesn't fail to entertain. Pushing the boundaries of violence and morality, and questioning religion and its use as an excuse to do horrendous acts in a crusade to exalt the Lord, we were testing our limits. Is it too much to kill a dog? How about if the dog tries to eat your candy corn friend? Are children off limits? We were also testing our teacher's limits. Would Mr. Cowgill draw the line? Or would he let our imaginations go wild? How much was too much? We had read many books – a number of them banned books – in his classes and it was clear to us that he was not a fan of censorship. But how far was too far? And would there be consequences? Would he turn one of us into the school counselor if we wrote something *too* fucked up?

The plot was never planned out. We opted instead to write by the seat of our pants. What was agreed upon, however, was the protagonist. As we sat in class brainstorming, Mr. Cowgill wrote our ideas on the dry erase board. Man – Leonard. Vigilante. Disgusted with commercialized holiday.

Easter. Rabbit, not man. There was our character. And that was it. Each week when we would meet, we were to read the chapter aloud and discuss. And with that, Mr. Cowgill handed out the chapter list with the due dates for each chapter and our first author went to work.

Editing was minimal when compiling this book, as I fixed only the punctuation and typographical errors, opting to leave the writing as in tact as possible to preserve the integrity of each author's original voice. What follows is by no means a masterpiece. The story meanders aimlessly for a bit and it is riddled with obvious plot holes. The writing is amateur to say the least. But it is an exercise in creativity. What is truly impressive, though, is the freedom that was given to us by Mr.

Cowgill, evidenced in the many boundaries we pushed. Disturbing, provocative, and at times, out right funny, this story is full of the dark fantasies from a truly unique group of small town kids from the Midwest.

Chapter 1

This morning when I awoke, fur glistening with droplets of sweat, dangling from every white strand, I thought of eggs. Damnable, cursed, off-white, ovular demons. They've spent years in His exalted throne, pilfering all of His glorious glory. Just three days until Good Friday, and where are all the crucifixes? Where are the throngs of wanton worshipers awaiting The J-Man's triumphant return? I'll tell you where! They're out buying

1

sugary confections and delicacies to stuff into their gluttonous, sinful mouths! They're traipsing about in spring hued sweater vests and khaki Dockers, ranting about flowers and cuddly little critters delivering baskets and baskets of hard-boiled SIN! And in the Lord's name? No! In the name of corporate greed! In the name of the flabby round buttocks of a modernistic, atheistic, consumer based society! To maintain the skewed portrait of a "Perfect American Family"!

But, alas, I am merely a pawn, blindly carrying out His plans, and it is not my place to question them. So I mustn't waiver from my duties, no matter how cruel or malicious they seem. I mean, is it really *murder* if A-O (Alpha and Omega) shines His magic light beam from outer space and decrees that *I* be His fluffy pale angel of death and destruction? Or is it merely religious cleansing? Either way, I have no say, control, or escape from this confounded conundrum. I only go to where the fetus lead, and do what *He* says to. This is why I loathe the poultry's unborn progeny so. They represent the finger of He Who Makest All, gracefully pointing at my unwitting and witless victims. I could not deny His orders, though it pains me so to carry them out.

So today, as with every other I can remember, I stood at the foot of my bed and carved little notches out of my chest. Scarlet droplets stained my ivory coat, as I listened for His voice, the sweet sound of serenity. His orders were a bit more profane than usual, and I protested meekly, as I always do.

"An entire fourth grade classroom, Lord? They'll name me insane! I mustn't! I'll fry, Lord, I'll fry! You think what they did to the Late JC was bad? Just wait! I will be begging for the nails!" I began packing my tools, and praying. "In the name of the Father..."

Beep. Beep. Beep. BEEP! BEEP! BEEP! Bang! Awake. What in God's name is that smell? I feel as if I've been sleeping for years. I am that smell. Shower. Wash away that filthy nightmare. Me a murderous zealot? Never. I'm already late for work. No time for product. Tasty organic carrot and I'm gone. I love my job. I really do. The people are

4

nice and don't seem to notice my…physical handicaps. Aside from my nocturnal subconscious wanderings, and my appearance, I am an average rabbit. I put my pants on one leg at a time like everyone else, except once I put my pants on, I have to make way for my cute, fluffy tail.

On my way to work in my Subaru Outback, I began to realize that I hate rush hour traffic. That is why I moved to Wyoming in the first place. To get away from all the hustle and bustle and bricca bracca of urban hell, and I just landed right back in it. I am the Co-Executive Vice-President of human resources at T.N.M.T.A.S.S. adhesive and tape factory. I have the esteemed responsibility of make sure the employees' needs are met, and their morale is high enough to keep our lines moving and production up. For example, I provide them with endless quantities of cakes, donuts, coffees, and teas. And, well…okay, that's all I do. But it is a very high stress job! It keeps me on my toes, and like my dear old second cousin's aunt's lover always said, "Leonard, there is no better place to be than on your toes!"

As the streams of vehicles began moving again, something caught my eye a couple rows up. Dangling from a man's rear view mirror, a little brightly colored egg. Something within me that I never let surface in my waking hours exploded with the sound of three twin ion engine fighters colliding mid-flight. I swerved around a plump middle-aged woman driving a van full of screaming toddlers and quickly caught up to my prey. He wore his hair in a disgusting comb-over, barely providing tiny bits of shade for his flaking scalp. His plaid shirt made me wretch and my eyes water. As I furtively followed barely a car length behind him, I reached into my glove box. I gently rested my now heavy hand in my lap. I followed. He drove on. I followed. Late for work. I followed. He sipped his coffee. I followed. "Now leaving Wyoming", a green sign spouted. Still, steady as a starving, slavering she-wolf, my pink tongue lolling, I followed.

Finally, his signal flashed, silently screaming, "Left! left!" I hung back, patient. So patient. We were in a seemingly deserted parking lot. Why had he picked this particular rest area to stop? It seemed fated, destined. Out of all the rest areas on this stretch of barren road, apparently devoid of any other life forms, why this one? I snickered to myself wryly and waited until he entered the men's restroom to exit my car. I checked my weapon, smiled at my reflection on the barrel, and listened closely to the sound the bullet made as it slid into the breach. The passenger door to his car was unlocked; a common mistake drowsy travelers often make. I reached toward the rear view mirror and tugged at the string that dangled the egg before me. Taunting me. As the door shut behind me, and I started making my way toward the bathroom, I could hear him whistling, and I recognized the tune. "Here comes Peter Cottontail, hopping down the…" I broke into a full-on sprint toward the commode, my .45 raised before me like a joust.

I ran down the line of stalls to the only one with its door closed. My foot raised, my knee bent forward, my joints aligned, and I put all my weight into a heavy kick that slammed the door into his nose. The cartilage splintered, giving off a sound I had never heard before, and it mixed in the air with his screaming and cursing. In my most gentle and kind voice I asked him to quiet himself so that I may speak.

"You're a damned maniac! You bust in here, break my nose, and ask me to keep quiet? Who the hell are you, and what the hell do you want?" He asked, as he pulled up his trousers and dabbed at his watering eyes, swabbing up blood with mounds of toilet paper. "I'm only going to say this once, so it would be in your best interest if you listened closely, you sick bastard. I have a gun in my car, loaded. And every bullet has something written on it. Do you know what they say? Hmmm?"

I grinned. "No, please enlighten me. What do they say?"

"They say 'attention: for use on crazy bastards who bust your face up and smile about it in a rest area men's room at two AM', that's what they say! Understand?!"

"Well, my bullets don't say anything except 'point four-five millimeter'. But my gun…" I raised my right arm and let the halogen's glow glisten off the chrome, "my gun is right here." He put his hands in front of his face like they were made of Kevlar, and whimpered something about kids at home, just wanting to go home, I don't know. I wasn't really listening. I was imagining what it must be like coming to terms with being shot down in a bathroom stall, on a bowl still full of your own feces. That must really suck. "Please, put your hands down, I am not going to hurt you. I swear."

He gave me a sidelong glance barely opening his squinting, teary eyes. "You swear?"

I put on my straightest face. "Yes, I swear." I lay my gun-filled hand gently across my heart. "I swear in God's everlasting name, I am not going to hurt you."

He lowered his hands. I shoved the chrome barrel under his chin and gave the stall a much needed paint job. His gray matter clung to everything, and my clothes were ruined.

"The only downside to murder: It's so messy." I picked what pieces of skull I could off my suit coat and walked out of the building. I walked to his car to check his story. I dug around like a pilfering thief, to no avail. "There's no gun here," I whispered to a man still sitting on a toilet bowl, head all over the stall, who couldn't have heard me, given the distance and volume of my voice. Oh, and the lack of a head. I got in my Outback, and headed home.

Beep. Beep. Beep. BEEP! BEEP! BEEP! Bang! Awake. The sky wept, dreary and overcast, when I sat up in bed and squinted out the window of my room. I always remember to draw back the curtains before I go to sleep every night. The morning sun helps to wake me up, like coffee for some. A sudden depression of mood. A vague memory, like a string of water-colored dreams. Flashes of red. The smell of gunpowder. An extreme close up of a muzzle stamp on an obese man's chin. Please, let it be just a dream.

I work for a tape and adhesives company. I help the floor workers maintain a euphoric state of mind, so as to keep up production. I hate my job, although most people do, so I won't elaborate. Freud said that we dream of things we wish to do in life, but will not allow our waking minds to even address. Our suppressed desires. I don't think I want to kill people. Was I even dreaming? Was Freud a quack? Many believe so. I guess I'll let myself be one of them, since it is blissful to be ignorant, and bliss is so very...blissful.

As I toweled dry after my shower, I thought ahead to the workday, and I realized something: I don't remember the last day that I did something for myself. Every afternoon for lunch I stop at this little café a block or so from work, have a mocha latte, and think about tomorrow. But every tomorrow is just the same as the day before yesterday's tomorrow. I mean, what is the point of looking ahead if it is the same as looking at *now*? If tomorrow is just today, repeated, then I could die today, and not have missed anything, right?

My boss didn't like my reason for missing work today. I could tell by the tone of his voice. He always sounds like he has a stick in his butt, yet today I could swear I heard it rubbing his uvula. It didn't sound very comfortable to say the least.

I have to get out of town. A tree, that's all I ask. I just want to see a tree. Okay, a group of trees would do nicely as well. Anything but concrete and steel. The city seems so drab, so barren, in spite of thousands upon thousands of people flurrying and fussing about. I have always been able to find solace in solitude. The woods have always given me both, so it is there that I must go. To clear my head. To sort things out. To think.

I pulled into the parking lot at The Mitharaan Woods recreational center and turned off my car, listening for the gentle hiss of the engine, as every little whirring piece slows to a halt, and it's sound dies away. The pebble-laden path into the forest led straight toward what looked like the gaping maw of a green Goliath, his chin on the

15

ground, waiting to devour me. I smiled and walked

gingerly in. I think he may have smiled back as I

turned around to watch the sunlight fade on the path

behind me.

Chapter 2

It would seem, as on a day like today, that with all of the moisture in the air, the soft ground sinks as a graveyard would. With all of the birds in the sky, waiting for a safe haven to emerge. The smell of freshness. Last night's rain had made this day a little more interesting. The road mirrors the sunbeams, shifting their position as the day drew to a close.

Timepiece reads 18:00 hours. Shortly the mark will be making his way through this mountain pass. Wyoming, one would think, would be dry, and perhaps a little cool this time of year, but at least dry. The ascent to my perch took longer than expected; I fell into thinking that maybe a sign was being made here. A wiser man would have merely broke down his rifle and made his way back to his car.

A wiser man would have decided against this from the moment that it was first proposed. Right there on a sunny morning at the local Starbucks on his side of the country. In good old Vermont. Conrad Beirut had beckoned his professional assistance on an ambush mission. Plan was simple enough, and the payoff was worth retiring at forty-two.

"So, you are here," Beirut stood with his right hand extended.

"So I am," I shook his hand, "Keep in mind though, this is the last time." The two men looked into each other's eyes and took their seats.

"I understand, who would want to keep up this savagery with this in the bank?" he passed a folded piece of paper across the table. I looked at Beirut as he smiled, his crooked teeth pressing his bottom lip further from his face than it already lay. The note, however, read $55.5 million. I remember that cold feeling passing through me at this instant. Who was this man I was to kill? "Tell me about it," I asked.

"Yes. One of our, how should I say, benefactors, has a cousin who had some trouble moving from Canada to America. He was detained in Wyoming - "

"Wyoming? He made it to Wyoming. Through Montana?"

"Aye, and is soon to be transported back into Canadian Custody. The man gave the authorities quite a chase through the Canadian Wilderness. The sort of altitude that he took as a route of escape is not properly guarded to say the least."

"You mean to tell me he took the Rocky Mountain pass from Canada through the great state of Montana, and then into Wyoming? And how was he captured, Beirut?"

"Coming into Wyoming, the more logical ways of escape had already been covered with Wyoming Police, County Police, State Police, and FBI. Storms have been too bad lately and helicopters at that altitude is not worth the loss, apparently. So, our man sat and thought about what was in his best interest, and a death-defying escape from the mountain into a fray of a considerable police entourage was not close to the top of the list. He gave himself up willingly to the Americans and knew that he would be shipped back into Canada for judgment. This mission is direct orders to our benefactor, to me, to you."

"Is this police escort a one-car move?"

"Hardly. I'm afraid that it is a three-car deal. You worried?"

21

Fifty-five and a half million dollars. The figure made so much of what I wanted out of this life possible. I had never made a trip out east to Thailand, or India. I have yet to see the Pyramids. I have been in Egypt, but I have never made it to Saqqara to see the massive step-pyramid of Zoser, or even been close enough to Giza's plateau to see the true pyramids of Cheops, Chephren, and Mycerenius. Some of the most terrific human achievements have been made in the world, and I have only but time to see them all if only I do this one last job. You do the math.

"Beirut," he set his ice tea on the glass table top, without moving his stare from my eyes, "what is the plan?"

Alas, I was not the wiser man. Money moved my mind to endless possibilities, on the far corners of the earth, and I am here now, in Wyoming, sitting on a rock, behind a larger rock, waiting for – what do we have here?

Seems to be a woman. She seems to be distraught, the way she's sloppily driving her Subaru Outback into the recreation center down the street. She squeals into her parking spot and slams the door shut. The air is so quiet; I can hear her talking to herself from where I sit. Something about eggs and Jesus?

I chuckle to myself, as I think how this lady with her problems and demons has no idea how serious the real world is about to get. She disappeared from sight en route the main path of

Mitharaan Woods just as the sunlight was fading to darkness. Shouldn't be too much longer until the designated caravan pulls through this quiet mountain pass.

I check my weapon one last time, I stare at the three bars of C4 planted on the side of two large pine trees with a half mile of possibility between them. The plan was, in fact, to create havoc and in the midst of confusion, take advantage of the perch and pull off six men in a matter of minutes.

Timepiece reads 18:29, won't be much longer now.

Birds fly into the air in the distance. There is the mark. I feel it, getting closer. The vibrations in the rock, I can sense the three cars approaching their final destination. Then they came into sight. One, two, three cars and four, five, six. Great. Not too big of a deal. No side streets around for alternate routes to be made by motorcar. Once on foot, shouldn't be too big of a deal, although, I must be patient. After the caravan moved past the first tree I had fixed C4 to, I blew them both, six cars trapped between a half mile of road and two monstrous trees now blocking their escape. The explosion brought the trees down just as planned, while the first car almost made it through the second tree before it hit, close only counts in horseshoes and hand grenades, and I'm down to five cars to take care of, position of mark is unknown so I must use supreme caution. Doubtful he was moving in the lead car.

The crazy lady is going to be wondering what the hell that sound was. I'm sure it shook the ground by where she was. I wonder if she's already on her way back to her car. I know she's freaking out.

I moved my crouched position slightly around the boulder and picked the first man to move out of his vehicle in the second car, then the first man to exit the sixth car. Headquarters was probably being notified at this instant of the ambush. All of the men below are in contact with one another, and I see all the men empty out except one car and that car pulls into the parking lot and parks on the other side of the crazy lady's Outback. As I take care of the men giving cover fire I see the mark run off into the woods with three men. Looks like they took off his ankle constraints to let them move faster, I'm sure.

I move from my perch, holding the rifle in my left hand, leaving my right free for balance. I move into the forest, but I think I'll take the path less taken and find out what we are dealing with here. Three cars, thanks a lot Beirut. I better be getting a bonus.

Almost nightfall here at 18:57. I give it a half hour before its pitch black. I have equipped night vision, actually two pairs. One for the mark, of his device of course. I am impressed, frankly, with how much planning went into this swift, destructive, yet efficient plan. How important is this man? I still don't know much about him.

I remember asking Beirut why this mark was so important. I said, "Beirut, why is this mark so important?"

"Come on now, you never asked questions before. Why are you so curious?"

"I suppose it is because this isn't my usual line of acquirement."

"Hmmm. I suppose I see what you are getting at, but I still don't think it is appropriate to discuss. Let me tell you his name, and if for some reason you know of this family then enough will have been said. And if you have not heard of this name in your time then it will not come as much of a shock when you do discover."

I remember being enthralled with who was about to be revealed. This legendary family he speaks so highly of. I know why they asked me, even though I was exclusively sticking with commercial hits at the time. Usually recovery

missions become too much work for the type of
regime of hired killers in which I belonged. I am
elite, and besides I make out fine without the mess
of getting so personal with targets.

"Valestri, Dimitri Valestri."

I had never heard his name in my time.
"Russian?"

"Aye. Now, Nathaniel, I know how much
you despise dealing with the Russians."

"Beirut."

"I know, watch him, but I assume he will act
within your designations."

The sun was gone. I sat upon a boulder, in
full lotus with my rifle balanced on my knees, eyes
closed, in intense meditation. Clearing my mind,
letting these five souls that are occupying the local

scene work against themselves. I grin as I thank

Dimitri for making sure I studied a topo of the land

before today. Since geology had always been a

hobby of mine, I decided to have some fun with it

and study. After all, I am a seasoned mountaineer.

When I was ten, my father and I climbed the

shield of El Capitan in Yosemite Valley in a day

and a half. We were on the valley floor by six

o'clock on day two. I miss my father. How many

ascents we made in the company of each other only.

The only time we had ever been accompanied was

in May of '99 when an upcoming GPS company

wanted the elevation of Everest measured. They

contacted my father who in turn immediately called

me. He was so excited to tell me. The company

even paid for these sherpa's to escort and help carry

the equipment. I recall the height we gathered from the summit of Everest was recorded at 29, 035 feet above sea level. This was interesting because the last measure of 29, 028 lapsed a seven feet differential. I ask myself, what's going on in the big picture that I can't see?

I hear a distinct crack in the distance and know that soon I should move into a better position. I don't have much time before back up arrives and besides, Mr. Valestri and I have a helicopter to catch at 20:00 hours in a clearing deeper in the recreation area. The plan was to fly once over at 19:00 hours over the pass, if no one was sighted, back off until 20:00 hours and meet at the clearing, if complications arose with that, all efforts to pick up were to be postponed until contact by Dimitri or myself via one of the two Nextel phones in my satchel. I traverse the trail in which the three men and my mark hike. They don't hear me thanks to the wetness preventing the crackling of leaves and brush. These men know I'm here, but don't know where. I stop behind one rather large tree and slip my rifle up to make a shot. First man down. Shot is very surreal here, I find that discovering a path that makes it through without touching a single tree is complicated, but possible, making it seem very much like a game. A very dangerous game. Second man down. Third man grabs my mark and pulls him in front of him like a shield. I silently congratulate him on discovering what direction the shot came from. The man held his ground. He had his weapon drawn. I put one in the left side of his ankle. He winced, but held his ground.

He fired a shot that stuck in the tree I was behind. He knew where I was. I am impressed. I stay silent, choosing to wait until this man does something. He holds his ground. Great, a hero. This may take some serious time, and I'm on a tight schedule to make this flight before I'm stuck here.

I hear something over the sounds in the forest. Something like a squeaking. So faint, it makes it difficult to discern what it is. I think to myself, "Can it be?" I grin and realize that destiny was turning in my favor. I only hope that the police officer I was dealing with was a man of honor. As the noise becomes easier to hear, I recognize the voice pattern, it is that woman who drives the

Subaru Outback. Wonderful! I thought she would have ran back after the blasts. She must not have heard them over her own ranting. Incredible.

As she moves in front of my tree, she does not notice the officer with my mark in front of him like a human shield. She cannot sense the tension here in the woods today. She is indeed too caught up with her everyday worries to even know what is going on.

"Ma'am, hold it. Back away from the tree," the officer warns her.

"Huh?" she stops dead in her tracks. I shuffle from behind my refuge and place the gun beside her head.

The situation just became more interesting. The police officer holding my $55.5 million mark as protection, as I stand twenty-five feet down the trail with a helpless citizen of the state. A police officer's worst nightmare. Let the negotiations begin.

Chapter 3

Wow, this is fantastic. All I wanted to do was go for a nice peaceful walk in the woods today, and now look at me. I am the hostage in what appears to be a very hostile situation.

The man with his rifle to my head says to the officer, "I don't want this to get any worse. I don't want to kill anyone else. All you have to do is just make an even exchange, the guy for the girl and I'll leave and go on my merry way."

"Of course, but what do you intend to do with this man after he is in your control?" replied the officer.

"I'm not at liberty to disclose this information, but I can tell you that you better stop with the questions and just hand him over or else things are going to get ugly."

"Okay, on the count of three, you put your gun down and allow the woman to come towards me and when she gets halfway, then I will let the man go."

"Okay, but if your man doesn't leave when she is halfway, the lady and you both die."

"Alright, one...two...three."

So there I was walking slowly towards the officer, when I got that feeling. You know the one you get when you know something is wrong. Well, as I glimpsed over my right shoulder just to make sure things were all right, I saw the man that had previously been holding me hostage looking down the barrel of his rifle that was pointed straight at my head. I had just enough time to somewhat sputter out an elongated "Noooooooooooooo," as the man pulled the trigger.

Then everything went into slow motion. I saw the bullet escape the end of the rifle barrel, spinning in its definite pattern heading straight towards my head. Closer and closer the bullet came and when it seemed as if it couldn't come any closer I winced, preparing myself for the blow, as much as a person can prepare before taking a bullet to the head. As the bullet hit me it made a noise one would

definitely not expect to hear at a time like this.

Beep. Beep. Beep. BEEP! BEEP! BEEP!

Bang! Awake. Ugh…I am drenched, completely

covered in sweat. It is a wonder I didn't drown

myself in all of it. Ah, a shower, that is what I need,

something to get this wretched stench and sweat off

me. Like usual running behind. Of course, no time

for breakfast, just my everyday usual, an organic

carrot. Then I hurriedly slip into my pants and take

the extra half-second to make a place for my cute,

fluffy little tail. Then out the door, into my Subaru

and on my way to my job, which of course I hate.

Who wouldn't? I mean I'm the Co-Executive Vice

President of Human Resources at T.N.M.T.A.S.S.

adhesive and tape factory. All I do there is deliver

the workers their cakes, doughnuts, coffees and teas. Why, without my services, the company would of course be destined to fail.

As I enter the lobby, my usual fifteen minutes late, I have to make up an excuse as to why I am late yet again to tell my boss, who, as usual, has a stick up his butt. Today I told him it was that I simply overslept, which he didn't believe or merely didn't care to buy. No big surprise to me; he has never believed that excuse since the day I brainstormed it up and tried it out for the first time.

I go to my office, which is in a corner, at the back of the factory. My office is very small. I've requested a bigger one ever since I got promoted to Co-Executive Vice President, but every time the President tells me there is no room to make me a bigger office. Besides it being small, it consists of three coffee pots, a cappuccino machine, and a doughnut maker for when supplies run low. Also, off in the corner sits my little delivery cart that was custom built for me by a co-worker named Fred. This aids me in delivering the workers their coffees, teas, cakes, and doughnuts. I also have a little desk that has a filing cabinet built into it and on top sits my Dell computer, which only has the basic programs: Microsoft Excel, Word, and a lot of games for when I'm done making my morning deliveries and waiting for morning break.

So, I go to my computer and print off the new, updated spreadsheet of what each worker's requests are for each break. Then I gather up the coffees, teas, cakes, and doughnuts according to the spreadsheet. I neatly organize them on my cart and head off.

First, I stop at Fred's station, which consists of Fred and three other workers. Their station does all the packaging of the tapes and adhesives and then puts the packages on the conveyer belt that leads to shipping.

"Here you are, Fred. Here's your French Vanilla cappuccino and two chocolate iced sprinkled cake doughnuts."

"Oh, thank you, Leonard, you are the greatest."

"Thanks, Fred. Do you have any changes that I need to make note of, or are you happy with your snack schedule?"

"No, I don't believe so. You have a nice day, Leonard, and I'll see you back here at morning break."

"Yes, same to you. Oh, and one more thing: the front right wheel on my cart is dragging a bit. Do you think you might have time to take a look at it at morning break?"

"Sure, I'll see what I can do."

So, with that I sat the three other workers snacks down, which were two regular coffees, a decaf coffee, and a couple of doughnuts. Now I was headed to shipping. The people at shipping are so rude. They don't appreciate a thing I do, which is no way to treat a Co-Executive Vice-President, but what is there to do?

Fred's men and the packing station are the best stop among my morning deliveries. Fred and I have been good friends since I first started working here. In fact, I actually worked for him at packing for a short while, then I moved on to inspecting, then to shipping, and then I got promoted to Co-Executive Vice-President of Human Relations. Fred and I would always go to the café together when I worked for him, but he says he just doesn't have time to go anymore and that the packaging requirements are becoming more demanding everyday. Nowadays we just have our little visits at each snack delivery and that is all the more we ever talk.

I usually finish my first snack delivery around 8:45 and today I managed to be about five minutes early. After this, I went back to my office and got in a couple good games of Solitaire before morning break. Then I got up, reloaded my cart and grabbed my list, and headed out to make yet another delivery of coffee and doughnuts. After morning break, I headed back to my office, updated the changes of the workers requests on my spreadsheet, and headed for the café a couple blocks from the factory, where I always eat lunch.

After lunch, I headed back to the factory, played a few more games on my computer and made my last snack break delivery. Then I added yet again more updates to the snack request list, cleaned out the coffee pots and cappuccino machine, and wiped off my delivery cart and put it back in its special little place. After all this, I then went and got into my Subaru and headed home.

On the way home, I remembered that for breakfast this morning I had the last of my carrots and that I needed to buy a couple more pounds to get by for the rest of the month. I decided I would go to the Wal-Mart about ten miles away from the factory. I walked in and was put into an instant outrage. All I saw were cute little Easter bunnies, which of course weren't as handsome as me, chocolate bunnies, sugar confection bunnies, cute little Easter egg decorations, and egg decorating kits.

The hell with all these people, all because some stupid ridiculous "American Tradition" just to be able to maintain the portrait of the "Perfect

American Family"! What is wrong with these people? Easter is about the rebirth of Christ. In what ways do giving each other cute little Easter candies and going on ridiculous rampages hunting for Easter eggs that I have to hide, which by the way, I am completely fed up with, have to do with the rebirth of Christ? Although, if the Easter bunny went on strike then, what do you think these outraged people would do? Of course, make a huge deal about there being no Easter bunny, and how horrible of a person I am. But do you think people would still remember that it was the day of the rebirth of Christ? No way! People don't even remember when I am around so what difference would it make if I did go on strike? Enough, I have to get my carrots so that I can make it home in time to catch the new episode of *American Idol.*

I walk to the produce section and find the carrots, weigh out five pounds, and head out to find one of the two cash registers that are open, even though the store has twenty. While in the check out line outraged, fools keep pouring in through the automatic doors heading straight to the Easter isles. Ugh…it truly disgusts me!

Finally, it is my turn to check out after a half hour. Oh, great. It's the same girl that always checks me out and makes some wise crack about me buying so many carrots and being in such a disgustful mood.

"How are you today, mama?" she asks.

"Just fine," I reply.

"Aren't you the - "

I stop her before she can continue. "Yes I am the woman that was in here last month buying an abundance of carrots."

"I thought you looked familiar."

"You always do."

My total came to eight dollars and ninety-three cents. I handed her a ten, got my change, and headed for the door. Then she had to say it.

"Hope you have a nice Easter!"

That did it! That sent me over the edge! She will be my next victim. All these fools and so hard to decide which ones to get rid of, but her, something about her, definitely her. She must go. I will wait for her until she gets off work, then I will track her down and do to her as I did to the unlucky bastard at the rest area.

That's the plan, a brilliant one at that. She will never expect anyone to be waiting for her in the parking lot. Luckily my .45 was still in the glove box and the box of bullets under my seat. She will see what happens to fools who are more worried about carrying on American tradition than focusing on the real meaning of holidays.

So here I sit in my Subaru Outback, my key turned just enough to allow the radio to play in the background, waiting and waiting. Roger Waters is quietly singing in my ear, "You gotta be crazy, you gotta have a real need. You gotta sleep on your toes, and when you're on the street, You gotta be able to pick out the easy meat with your eyes closed. And

then moving in silently, down wind and out of sight,
You gotta strike when the moment is right without
thinking." And I remember why I love Pink Floyd.
This song may be called 'Dogs', but to me, it's
'Rabbits'. And I sit, waiting until the unfortunate
girl will get off work and innocently walk to her
car. Then she will be mine. I will get her, and then
no more worrying about her annoyance when I go
to buy my carrots and one less idiot walking around.

Ten o'clock, still no sign of her. Eleven
o'clock, still nothing. Twelve o'clock, what, is this
a girl? A girl leaving from the exit of Wal-Mart. Is
it her? Yes, it is her. Now the time has come. I must
activate my plan.

Chapter 4

As I sat in my car, I cautiously watched the girl cross the store's parking lot, contemplating my next move. I mean, is she worth all that hassle? Should I waste my last few bullets today? The earlier scenario played in my head like a never-ending tape reel, "Have a nice Easter....Have a nice Easter!" I had my gun resting in my lap fully loaded, waiting for the perfect opportunity. I thought to myself, this is neither the place nor time to commit another murder. There are way too many people bustling about.

As she approached her car and got ready to place her belongings in the back seat, I noticed a bumper sticker reading T.N.M.T.A.S.S. stuck to the back window of her red Mitsubishi Eclipse. I thought to myself, why does she have this decal posted? Was she an employee of the company? No, that could not be possible, as I had never come across her while making my rounds. Or maybe she is related to an employee? That had to be the case.

I decided to hold off on my plan and follow her until I figured out exactly whom she was related to at the factory. I started my engine once she backed out of her parking space. She was several cars away from me, so I began to inch out of my spot cautiously. At the parking lot exit, she made a left followed by a quick right. I hurriedly did the same, trying to stay a few cars back and out of sight. She continued down the road until we approached a huge sign reading Royal Harbor Estates, where she stopped and made her final turn. The homes were mainly large, two-story Tudor and colonial style residences. There was a private community pool, as well as a clubhouse and a recreation area. Apparently, she was of relation to a wealthy figure from the company. But who could it be? I had to find out.

I parked in a cul-de-sac adjacent to the driveway and watched closely as the woman began to gather her bags and leave the car. This was the perfect opportunity to carry out my plan. As I reached for the door handle, with my gun in my right hand, it occurred to me. The man who greeted her at the door was my boss. Why just kill the one who only insulted me once in the store, when I could kill the boss as well? I mean, he insults me everyday, and without him, there would be no indecision of hating or loving my job. All I need now is a plan to eliminate the two of them. This is wonderful!

On my way home, I recalled the dream I had the night before. It was obvious the gunman that took me hostage was my boss. Not only was he there to kill the other people in the dream, which obviously represented T.N.M.T.A.S.S. employees, he was there to kill me; trapping us between two trees, so he could come in for the kill. Without him, it was evident I would get better reception from God, and no longer have these confusing dreams, allowing me to fulfill the tasks He assigns.

While at home, I sat down in my rocking chair sifting through several brilliant scenarios. Whatever means I decide to do them in, I want it to be fairly long lasting, and hopefully painful, so shooting them in bed was not an option. Then I thought, why not send them a package through mail with a bomb enclosed? The problem with this idea is it might kill only one rather than both, and besides, it would be way too quick. Perhaps a basket full of chocolate rabbits filled with rat poison would do the trick? Or maybe I could cut the brake cables in their car? No, no, these ideas won't work. But the car…that had potential. I got it!

I went to work the next day full of hope that my plan would work. I got my first indication that it might when I overheard my boss talking to a manager about the great deal he got to visit a timeshare condo for free the following weekend in the Santee Mountains.

"Yeah, this guy called me and wanted to know if I would like to visit this place for free. I have a weekend of relaxation and all I have to do is listen to some guy talk about buying a timeshare in the condo for about an hour. I don't plan on ever buying it, but it will give my wife and I a chance to just hang out over the Easter weekend," he said.

"Sounds great! When do you plan on leaving?"

"Oh, we are going to take off on Friday morning around 8:00. We are hoping to arrive around noon, just in time for a nice romantic lunch."

That was just the news I needed to hear. I had to go back to my office and phone my uncle to thank him for the invitation I arranged for my boss. I could tell my boss was real pleased with his weekend of fun. Over the next several days, I went through the workday cheerfully, knowing he and his insolent wife would soon be leaving us. What a most fitting time it would be to dispose of them over such an unfortunate holiday.

On Wednesday night after work, I went home and began to carry out my plans. First, I boiled half a dozen eggs. Next, I carefully peeled the shell coating off of them and placed them in the refrigerator overnight. The next day I went to work, hoping this would be the last time I ever saw my boss.

Thursday night came. It was time to put my plan to work. I carefully placed the eggs in a basket and took them to my car. I got in and started to back out of the driveway hoping that all would go according to plan. I parked my car in the same cul-de-sac, approximately 100 feet from my boss's front door. In the driveway stood the two cars. I cautiously looked around to make sure no one was out during these late hours. Not a soul in sight. I grabbed the basket of eggs and quietly opened my car and got out with it. Gently, I closed the door. As I started advancing towards the drive, a dog barked.

I froze, but was only momentarily scared. Even if someone looked out a window they would probably not see me through the shrubs and trees that surrounded these upscale houses. Fortunately, the animal stopped barking, it probably had smelled rabbits before and realized that it could not catch one. So I again proceeded towards the cars. Peering inside the minivan, I spotted the already packed luggage in the backseat. I smiled to myself, thinking how my boss thought he would be going on this wonderful vacation. I went to the back of the vehicle, reached into the basket, and pulled out an egg, stuffing it into the tailpipe. Fortunately, the tailpipe was big enough not to offer much resistance. I pulled out another egg and did the same. Then a third, and a fourth. I tried a fifth, but it would not go in. I did not want to force it and leave

behind smashed egg residual, which could give

away my plan: to kill them by carbon monoxide

poisoning. What a wonderful, and simple idea this

was, and so fitting for the Easter holiday. I stood up,

and turned around to start walking back to my car,

when the dog started barking again. I looked around

the neighborhood, still no lights. The coast was

clear. I again continued to walk to my car and

silently got in. I proceeded to go home and

imagined what the local headlines would read the

next morning. "Vacationing Couple Killed When

Car Slides Off Rugged Mountain Road."

I went to bed once I got home, tired from all

the excitement of my plan. I began to dream that the

Big Man approved of my scheme. I awoke the next

morning at about 8:30, deciding to take a quick drive by my boss's house. Before I left, I phoned work and left a message that I would probably be late. I brought along a pair of binoculars and my morning carrot. Sure enough, they had left. I smiled to myself and thought maybe I would be lucky and could see them winding up the mountain from the vantage point of a rest stop located at the bottom of the mountain.

Mr. Snyder and his wife sat silently for the first half hour of the trip. They had skipped their morning coffee and breakfast due to a late morning start, and were not quite awake yet. They had already encountered the first switch back and were now heading to the second when Mr. Snyder yawned and commented to his wife.

"The car seems a little sluggish this morning."

"Perhaps it is due to the cold weather," she replied.

"Thank goodness the heater is working though."

Ah, there they are. They haven't made too much progress, but they are moving and obviously they have no idea that they are slowly gassing themselves to death. I should be able to watch them for the next ten or fifteen minutes switching back along the mountain road before I lose sight of them. Maybe I should follow them? What a wonderful vision it would be to see their car smashed at the bottom of a ravine! What a happy Easter that would be!

"I sure don't seem to be able to wake up this morning," said Mr. Snyder.

"Neither do I," his wife replied.

"Ah, but we will be there soon. We'll have a wonderful lunch when we arrive and not have a care in the world for the next couple of days."

After pulling out of the rest area, I headed up the mountain for a couple miles observing the evergreen trees, large boulders, and the steep precept over the edge of the road. As I looked down the steep valley, I congratulated myself on my brilliant plan. Even if they don't successfully run off the rugged road, oncoming traffic ought to do the trick when they begin swerving. And I know he is not the type of person to pull over, whatever the reason, when he is determined to reach a goal.

As I was climbing, I took note of the time and realized it was getting late. I told the assistant manager I should arrive for the day around 11:00, and I did not want anyone to be suspicious of me. Before arriving, I decided to stop by a little vegetarian café at the bottom of the mountain and treat myself to a tall glass of carrot juice, carrot cake, and a cucumber sandwich. I could only imagine the Snyder's now getting drowsier and drowsier every foot they went up.

"Did you pack any coffee in the thermos? I am beginning to feel a little dizzy," Mr. Snyder remarked.

"No," she replied, "It must be the altitude, and not having any breakfast. I am beginning to feel a bit lightheaded myself."

"Whoa! I started swerving into the other lane a bit," Mr. Snyder exclaimed. "I just need to be more careful. It's not too much further, so let's keep going."

I arrived at work at half past ten and began to prepare the employees midmorning snacks. I realized I had to act nonchalant. Once I started making my rounds, with a calm expression on my face, I could see the story in front of my eyes. Tragedy Over Easter Weekend, but to me it was anything but a tragic holiday.

Chapter 5

I was nothing short of a God at my work. I started at 10:00 AM and finished at about 10:45 AM. 'Damn, I am good', I thought to myself as I sat in my small, cramped office, clicking mindlessly away. Haha. By this time that piece of trash boss of mine and his annoying wife should be softly slipping into a dream-like state as they ramp themselves off a cliff to their crushing oblivion.

I left work, excited to get home, turn on the news, and see pictures of my boss and his wife's burned, mutilated bodies lying lifelessly next to their piece of crap foreign car. Haha. It makes me giddy just thinking about it. I finally arrived at my typical suburban home at 6:00 PM. My house is nothing exciting, in fact it is rather bland. It has a small kitchen, one bedroom, a bathroom, and one chair that sits three feet in front of my television. The first thing I did was take off my shoes, go into the kitchen, open my broke down fridge and take a drink of milk that has been sitting in there for months, just a little chunky. After I drink my cottage cheese, I go sit in my chair and turn the TV to the news station. WHAT? No mention of my boss being horribly maimed or being ravaged by a

70

fire from the wreck. I can't believe this crap! I decided to lie in my bed and wonder what happened. What went wrong? Maybe they haven't been found yet. Yes, that's what happened, they just got horribly mutilated; no explosion and they are being pecked apart by some sort of small woodland creature. Haha. Hopefully a rabbit like myself, a savage man-eating rabbit.

I wake up to a blood-curdling scream. Where did that come from? Was that me? I wander into my bathroom and ponder when and how my life became so complicated and harsh. I can pinpoint it to one event. When it found me. He came to me in the season of Samhain. It told me to call him "Dante". I had never heard a name like that

71

before – sounded French or very old. Either way, it was bad news.

Dante was a friend who understood every thought I had; it was like he was some sort of higher power. Sadly, as fast as he came into my life, he was gone and I didn't hear from him again till a couple days ago. When I woke from that horrible dream about murder, I walked into my bathroom and took my pill as usual. When I turned around to walk out of my bathroom, there he was in all his glory just lying on the floor next to my bathroom door, glowing with a dulled presence. This was the first time I saw him in almost three years. When I was younger, he was the soothing voice that consoled me when my parents were mysteriously murdered and were hid in the basement of our home. After I got over the initial shock of him just re-appearing, I asked him where he had been.

"Follow me, young one. Everything will be explained in time," he responded. Where he had in mind, I had no clue, but it was completely unexpected.

To my shock and amazement, he led me to a quaint little sweets shop that is open all hours of the night. The shop was all dressed up for the Easter holiday. It was enough to make me sick, seeing all the chicks, rabbits, and sugarcoated sin that is suppose to represent the day of Jesus. When I saw all this 'unification' and 'tolerance' of man, I couldn't help but think that this is ridiculous.

As I looked on at all the sinners teaching their children the ways of evil, Dante softly whispered, "These small trivial things will be their damning. Do you understand?"

"Yes, these small treats blur the vision of the righteous, thus they are losing the true reason for why all this has come about. But what can I do?"

"Become the angel of his vengeance," he replied calmly. I allowed a devilish smile to spread across my face. Haha. Angel of vengeance – has a strange ring to it.

The next day I called off work so Dante could teach me everything he knew, such as how to kill a fully grown man with one hand while keeping the other over their mouth. I woke up to get ready for my lesson of the day and Dante told me that we were going to work today because I had to see something. Wonder what it could be? I stuck

Dante's tiny brown, orange, and white triangular body into my front breast pocket of my sleek black Gucci business suit. I made room for my cute bunny tail then put on my usual attractive amount of makeup and slipped on my black DKNY three-inch high heels. I stared at myself in the mirror. God, this outfit made me look extraordinarily sexy. After I pulled my medium length bunny ears back into a bun, I left my house and got into my Subaru Outback and headed off to work still wondering what was so damn important. I would soon find out.

When I arrived at work, my friend Cadance ran up to me with an excited face. She exclaimed, "Oh my God, did you hear?" in the giddiest voice I had ever heard.

"What?" I asked.

"Someone shoved hardboiled eggs in the tailpipe of Maleficent," she stated. Maleficent was the nickname for our boss and let me tell you it was a damn good name for that ass.

"Really?" I replied with 'surprise'. "What happened?" I excitedly asked. I had completely forgot about my untraceable murder of the boss till Cadance brought it up.

The moment she paused to take a breath seemed to last at least an hour. In that short period of time a thousand different scenarios flashed through my head. All of them made me smile, except one – that he had survived somehow.

Cadance finally responded. "Well his wife said she was getting woozy so he pulled over and left the car running and when she got back in she immediately passed out. So he pulled her out and woke her up and then he called for help."

"What? What happened after that?" I blurted out in a panic.

"Well, when the ambulance got there they loaded her in and he got in with her and they went to the hospital."

WHAT? What about the freaking car? I thought. "Well what happened to the car? I mean, how did they find the…eggs?" I asked as if I had no idea what was going on. Haha.

"The craziest way. I guess some guy saw the car still running jumped in and took off, they found the car at the bottom of a huge ravine with the guy strung out in pieces."

"How did they find out about the eggs?" I timidly asked.

"Apparently the boss paid big bucks to find out what happened, and they found the eggs crammed in the tailpipe. Isn't that crazy? Especially with it being so close to Easter."

"Yeah, that is crazy. Do they have any idea who did it?" I worriedly asked.

"Haha, that's really funny Leo, no clue," Cadance replied.

"Is the boss here today?" I asked.

"No, but I guess he is coming in later to get some files and stuff so he can keep up while his wife is in the hospital."

After I finished talking to Cadance, I started my work and got done quicker than usual. I guess

fear makes people do extraordinary things. I was
scared to death that someone might have seen me
do my deed. When I finished I went into my office
and closed the door. I needed help. I pulled Dante
out of my pocket.

"Dante, what should I do? They are going to
find out it was me," I asked the small piece of stale
Halloween candy.

Dante replied, "Do not fear, young one, no
one knows, and do not worry that your plan failed,
another opportunity will present itself." I finished
my work and left.

On the way home Dante didn't say a word.
It was like he was thinking or getting a message
from God. When we got home, Dante said
something that was muffled by the pocket where he

was held. I pulled him out and asked him what he said as I walked into the house. He asked the weirdest question.

"You have a gun, don't you, Leonard?" he asked.

"Well yeah, the one I keep in my car to kill fools. Why?"

Dante insisted, "Get it! It's time me and you do something about this bastard holiday."

I had to ask, "Get it? What for?"

"You are the angel of vengeance, right?" Dante inquired.

"That's what you say I am to God," I replied.

The piece of candy shot back, "Your damn right child, its time you show His wrath. Now get the gun!"

I changed out of my work clothes into a pair of black cargo pants with a black shirt. I put on my long black coat and perked my fluffy bunny ears up. I got back into my car. The gun was just where I had left it, in my glove box. It was such a pretty piece of modern death with its shiny chrome and dull black handle. It was a .45 caliber semi-automatic pistol with a clip that holds fifteen rounds. I had re-loaded it earlier with hollow points mostly because I like what they do. You shoot someone with a regular bullet, yeah, it will do the job, but you blast someone with a hollow point and it will look like a knocked over garbage can behind an Italian restaurant.

I started the car up and asked, "Where are we going? Who are we going to make an example out of?"

Dante replied, "Stop at this rest area."

Rest area? That word set me off. I began having flashbacks of brutally gunning down men at rest areas in the middle of the night. At the rest area, I sat and waited. I felt like I was in another dream. Haha. Oh, here comes a car. I laid down in my seat until I saw the lights die. I put on my cute bunny face and exited my vehicle and walked past his.

Oh my God! The dangling egg from my dream. I continued toward the bathroom. I ran into the bathroom and kicked the stall door and it slammed into his face. Haha. His nose busted. Then

he looked up at me and I knew him. Haha. It was

my boss, how nice.

He knelt before me, his face shattered,

oozing blood and asked in a panicked voice, "What

the hell are you doing kicking my face in and why

are you wearing that stupid bunny mask?"

All I could say was, "Why are you wearing

that stupid human mask?"

He looked at me like he didn't understand

that I am a rabbit. How could he miss the cute, little

fluffy bunny tail and the big floppy ears? Maybe the

blast to the face by the stall door had blurred his

vision. As he sat on his knees and pondered what I

just said I took the pause to put my gun to his

forehead and spray the back of the stall a reddish

gray color. I stood and looked at the body, waiting

for the blare of my alarm clock to wake me up, but

it never came. So, I went to my car, drove home,

and went to sleep.

Chapter 6

I woke up this morning with the biggest grin on my face. Pleasure bubbling and oozing throughout my soul like hot lava from a volcano. I replayed the events from last night over and over in my head like a motion picture. Every time it came to the part where I pulled the trigger, a faint little chuckle escaped from my chapped, dry lips. All I could think about was the grayish red color spattered on the wall. Maybe I should become an artist, I thought to myself.

I decided to stay home today and just lie around and do nothing. As I was flipping through the television, something revolting and hideous was on channel 9. The Easter Day Parade gatherers made their trek across the streets of New York City. My blood began to boil and my face turned flushed pink. Damn all those people and their sinful celebration. But as the day progressed on, I couldn't help but have this little feeling of unhappiness, like something was missing. I tried and tired to figure out what exactly it was, and then it hit me like a ton of bricks. The bastard's wife was still alive. As far as I knew she was still in the hospital, so I decided to pay her a little visit.

The smell of St. Jude's hospital was enough to make me want to vomit. The mixed smell of stale urine and sanitizers filled my nostrils and burned my nasal passages. I went to the clerk's office and asked Mary if she could please tell me where Delia Snyder's room was.

"Oh, Mrs. Snyder, man I feel really terrible for her, losing her husband and all. It's crazy how sick people are these days. I mean, whose heart would be black enough to shoot a man at a rest stop? Psychos."

"Yes indeed, it is quite sad. In this day and age you never know people anymore. The very person you cut off on the highway, or the person behind you at McDonalds, or even the very person you are talking too could be a cold-blooded killer,"

87

I said. Mary just gave me this dazed and confused look and said Delia was in room 1225.

Looking at Delia's pale, wrinkle-ridden face, I began to feel sorry for her….no, maybe not. Her dreary, droopy eyes showed signs of few hours of sleep. As I walked in the room, she looked up, startled.

"Um, yes, can I help you?" she asked quietly.

"I just wanted to stop by and give my condolences."

"Thank you very much, but may I ask how you know my husband and I?"

"Me and your husband were old college buddies, and we grew up in the good old mean streets of Omaha," I replied, lying my butt off. "So how are you feeling Mrs. Snyder?" I asked, while the whole time I was thinking, 'I want you dead, and soon.'

"It's been pretty tough. We had been married ten years and then to lose the baby really topped it all off."

"The baby?" I asked.

"Yes, I was three and a half months pregnant, and now she is gone."

"I am really sorry to hear that. Well I have to get going, but I hope you get better soon."

"Thank you very much," was her only response.

I disappeared out of the hospital and hopped into my Subaru, trying to think of the different ways I could kill Mrs. Snyder. I needed help and I needed

it fast. Who could I turn to? Who else but Dante!
When Dante spoke to me it was like the heavens
parted and that angel woman began to sing. Dante
was my mentor, but more than that, he was like the
father I never had. When he had something to say, I
listened. When he said hop, I asked how high. I
reached into my left shirt pocket that covered my
pearly, soft fur and my heart froze momentarily.
Where was he? Then I remembered I forgot him on
my nightstand next to my bed.

On my way home I stopped at Wal-Mart to
pick up a few things – carrot cake and juice to name
a few. As I walked throughout the store, I saw those
damn Easter decorations and it made me sick. How
dare they mock me and put my wonderful face on
chocolate bars for these ignorant little fools to

enjoy. I had to leave immediately. I sped away

thinking only of Dante and how much he was going

to help me.

I walked in the house and immediately

sought out after the Great Almighty One. And there

he was, right where I had left him. I asked him how

I could kill the old hag. His reply was to hook up a

bomb to her car, but I quickly put an end to that

idea because it was too quick and too messy. I

thought, and thought, and thought, and then I finally

came up with the greatest plan to make her 'sleep'

forever.

Once again I was on my way to a lovely

hard day of work. It might not seem like it but

delivering coffee, and doughnuts, and tea to the

employees is very hard work. I mean, all day I am

like their little rabbit slave. Leonard, do this, and Leonard, do that. It is pretty stressful. All day I am up and down the great elevators tending to people's wants. And for what, a measly little paycheck? I hated my job but someone has to do it, so it might as well be me. All they talked about in the office was Mrs. Snyder and how sad it was the Mr. Snyder was killed so viciously. As for right now they had no suspects, and they were trying to follow every possible lead they could, but let's just say they weren't rolling in. It was ironic that at work, I had to put on this mask of sympathy and act like I was so sad, knowing in my head the truth. Knowing I was the one who murdered Mr. Snyder. That has a nice sound to it, doesn't it – I murdered Mr. Snyder, and now I was going to do the same to his poor innocent little wife. Ha! The day went surprisingly quick, considering all the work I had done. On the way out, Rob Barker asked would I like to go out with him and have a few drinks. I politely declined with intentions to smooth out the last wrinkles of my brilliant plan. My plan was so perfect, nothing, and I mean nothing, could go wrong. They won't even be able to think of a suspect.

This morning I awoke to the sun pouring in through my dirty cracked blinds, and the birds making entirely too much noise. I started my morning off right with a nice hot, steamy shower. Man, it felt good to let my ears down and the feeling of that hot water running through my fur was like heaven. After my shower, I settled at the kitchen table for a nice little breakfast. I was going to need my energy because I had a full day ahead of me, but an even more exciting night. After breakfast, I watched the television to see what was going on in this god-awful world nowadays. And, of course, every commercial and every show and station devoted its time to sharing with us the joys of Easter. This is the one time of the year where I wish these ignorant little fools would really get what they deserved. I wish they knew what it was like to feel unappreciated and commercialized. These maggots have forgotten the real meaning of Easter. It's no longer about Christ, but about stupid little egg hunts and those retarded marshmallow delights. When is this world going to change? No telling where we will be in ten years if these idiots keep this up!

At around noon I decided to go to the mall. I had not been shopping in quite some time and I thought it would relieve some of my tension. My two new black ski masks looked great and I knew they would be useful tonight. I also purchased a pair of black sweatpants and some black leather gloves. All these items were essential to the special evening I had planned. I spent the rest of the afternoon cooped up in my room, going over every little detail so everything would be perfect to a T. I then began a brief conversation with my good old buddy.

"So Dante, do you really think this plan of ours is going to be as easy as we think?"

"Of course it will, why wouldn't it? I hope you are not getting second thoughts about it, because if you are, you better get your head right."

"No, I'm not having second thoughts, its just as though this plan seems too perfect."

"Of course it seems too perfect; it's really quite simple. It's not messy, but yet it gets the job done."

So about five hours later I was in my room getting dressed and getting ready to rock and roll. At exactly 9:52 PM, I was getting in my Subaru and speeding towards the hospital. At 10:16, I was circling the parking lot looking for a place to park. I found a spot and sat in the car for a few to gather my materials and get ready. I patted my breast pocket making sure Dante was there.

"I am here, Leonard. You know what you have to do, and you know it's the right thing to do, so get in there and do it."

"You're right," I replied. "How many times have I done this? I'm ready."

I entered the hospital from a rear door that was conveniently left cracked open. I went up the emergency stairs to the twelfth floor. Once I was at the door, I peered around making sure no one was watching. Once I saw that it was all clear, I carefully made my way to room 1225. As I peered in, I saw that a nurse was in the room checking up on her. Quickly, I darted into the men's restroom right across the hallway. I stayed in there until I heard Mrs. Snyder's door close and the nurse's footsteps walking away. When I thought the coast was clear, I tiptoed into her room and stood over her bed watching her sleep. Suddenly all kinds of emotions began to rip through my body. I felt rage, hatred, and a sick, sadistic kind of happiness all at once. I stood there watching her chest move up and down, up and down. Then I was snapped back into reality by the voice of Dante asking me what I was waiting for. I began to make my way over to her bedside. I pulled out the machine that would end her life forever. I grabbed the two paddles, turned the dial to the highest number that I thought would do the trick, and pressed the button. Bam! The electricity shot throughout her body and flung it helplessly into the air off the bed. No flat line yet. Once again I shot another dose of the lethal electricity, and still she would not go. Damn her, I thought, why won't you die? I turned up the power five more notches, then I let loose. That was the killer. As I watched her vital sign go flat across the screen, a blanket of joy wrapped around my body.

Quickly, I ran out of the room and right back down

the stairs. Right before I descended, I turned around

in time to see three nurses rushing into Mrs.

Snyder's room. You are too late, I thought to

myself.

As I sat in my Outback and just thought

about what had happened, a boisterous laugh

erupted from the depths of my soul. I pulled into my

driveway and walked to my room knowing I was

going to sleep peacefully tonight.

Chapter 7

Just as I knew I would, I slept wonderfully last night. Not once did I wake up from those terrible dreams I've been having. Just knowing that I've gotten rid of the boss and his wife puts a tranquil feeling over my entire body. So, I think to myself, what should I do today?

I sit up and turn on the TV to check the morning news. High of sixty-three and sunny. I can already tell today is going to be a lovely day.

Oh, great, what is this? I'm on TV! What an idiot. Of course, the hospital has surveillance cameras. Well, at least I wore my black ski mask. I should be okay. I'm okay. I need Dante. I frantically jump out of bed and start searching for my sweet candy friend. My coat pocket? No. My pants pocket? No. The bathroom sink? No. Where the hell could he be?

"Dante. Dante! DANTE!!!"

"Leonard, Leonard. It's okay. Everything is okay, I'm right here." He was exactly where I had left him the night before. He had been sleeping on top of the TV. "What's all this yelling about?"

"Didn't you see? I'm on TV. They got me on camera. It's all over now. It's just a matter of time before they catch us. First, we're on the news, and then they find the witnesses. Before you know it, all of a sudden, we will be relaxing one morning, minding our own business, being the law-abiding citizens that we are, and BOOM! All of the sudden there they are at the front door to arrest us."

"*Us?* I didn't do anything."

"Oooh no. Don't even try that again. It was your plan. Remember, 'what are you waiting for'? I'm not taking the blame for this one. You were the mastermind behind it all. You're the one who didn't even *think* about the cameras."

"Ha! I can see it now: 'Man Says He's Framed By A Small Piece of Candy'. Well, I guess at least you could plead insanity."

"Yeah right, Dante, we both know that I'm not nuts."

"I know, I know. Let's go for a walk. We need some fresh air."

I got up and got dressed. I decided to go about my business as usual. There's nothing I can do now but wait and hope that it all blows over without me on the suspect list.

Changing my train of thought, I realize for the first time this year, it's spring. I love spring because when it's fifty degrees outside in the spring, you don't need a jacket. Sometimes you might even wear shorts. But when it's fifty degrees in the fall, everyone gets out their winter coats. I always feel so good in the spring when I finish shedding all my winter fur. Really, right now, I'm at my prime. Handsome as a fox. I wash my fur with that luxurious Herbal Essence stuff, and by the time

I get out of the bath, no rabbit within a thirty-mile radius can even dare to try to resist me.

We decided to go to the park for a change of environment. Usually I try to avoid the park, but I was feeling especially sexy. The thought was crossing my mind that maybe I would find The One today: the rabbit of my dreams. I had been trying to keep my mind off of the events of yesterday. The very same events that had brought me so much inner-peace and serenity were now causing me to be close to a breakdown.

So Dante and I go to this park about ten minutes down the road, Hewitt's Creek Park. I've never understood why they call it that because I don't know of any creeks, rivers, or streams around here. All they have at this park is a little play area for the kids: brightly colored swings and slides, sand, and the usual bit of stuff. Then they have picnic tables and benches for the parents to sit at. And there is a sidewalk for people to jog and walk on. Dante and I go for the path.

The whole time we're walking I feel unable to completely relax. When I first start trying to stop thinking of the events of the past day, I think of a time about a year ago. This is the reason that I often try to avoid the park. There are always so many people out there walking their dogs and minding their own business. But really, they never know when their lousy mutt is going to decide to attack me.

Believe me, I've been there. I've seen it happen. And really, I'm surprised it doesn't happen more often. Dogs must be becoming so domesticated that they don't even have their natural instinct to hunt anymore.

I was at a park very similar to this one when some crazy mutt attacked me. I wasn't too terribly surprised. I'm just happy they passed those leash laws here so the dog couldn't even get a good hold on me. Since then, I have often opted not to go to large open areas with several different types of dogs. Under normal circumstances, I would be too afraid, and I've always been told that dogs can smell fear.

As I'm thinking of my terrible history in parks, once again, my thoughts turn back to last night. I can't relax. I think to myself, 'They know everything.'

Just as I'm about to scream, "Yes! It's me! I'm the cruel, cold-blooded killer," I reach my hand into my pocket and pull out little Dante for a bit of self-assurance. At this time, I really needed some confidence.

I wasn't ready for what would happen.

At the exact same moment that I pulled Dante out, he took a suicidal jump from my fingertips to the hard, cold concrete path. And just as he fell to the pavement, this monster of a dog and his disgustingly obese owner carelessly stroll by.

Before I can do anything, before I can speak, move, think, or even breathe, Dante is on this mutt's tongue. I leap at this disgusting disgraceful mess of a pet. But, it's too late. Dante is already on his way down this dog's esophagus, heading straight to his stomach to be digested and forgotten for the rest of my life, for all of eternity.

But NO! I can't let this happen. Dante is my only true friend. Dante is my soul mate, my companion. He is my pride, my joy, my life! I think of all of this so quickly that I don't even realize it until I look back. I only leap at the dog. I take the collar and I run. Or, at least I tried to run. But, like the owner, this dog is quite obese. I was struggling for some time when I finally realized what was going on. Everyone in this park had completely stopped what they were doing. There was absolutely no movement except for my struggling cries to get this dog out of the public eye.

Self-control, I tell myself. I cannot do this here. But it looks as if I may have to. I know exactly what I have to do. I have to rip this dog open and carefully slice his stomach to save Dante. Just not here, anywhere but here. It's too late now to try the calm, gentle approach. Everyone's eyes are on me. Now is the time to make the escape, or I might not have another chance.

As I glance around for a way of escape, I spy the old stone bathrooms by the spiral slide. I think to myself, 'If I move quickly, I may be able to throw this dog over my shoulders and make it to the bathroom before they all come to.' Mostly everyone at the park is completely shocked and stuck. No one has made a single attempt to save this dog. The owner hasn't even tried anything. Fatty ran like a scared little bitch as soon as he saw me leaping towards him.

'Maybe,' I think to myself, 'Maybe if I keep my head down, no one will even remember my face.'

I always try to think optimistically when I'm committing some sort of 'terrible' crime. So, I just go for it. I pick up the monstrous killer, throw him over my back, and run like hell towards that small, secluded bathroom. I really, truly did not think I was going to make it. I really, for one second, thought I was done for.

But, I did it. I made it. As soon as I got into the bathroom, I put the dog in front of the doorway. Man, did I get lucky that the door opened in from the inside. Otherwise, I would have had the whole crowd in the bathroom with me trying to give this dog the careful surgery he needed.

As soon as I got situated in the bathroom, I realized once again, I don't have time to lose. Dante could be anywhere right now. He could be stuck in the throat. He could be traveling down the esophagus. He could be digesting in the stomach. He could even be getting ready to pass through the intestines already.

I knew the first thing I had to do was kill the dog. In all of my panic, I completely forgot about my small pocketknife that my nephew got me last summer when he went to Switzerland. So, in a state of desperation, I grabbed the long, steel nozzle of the sink and ripped it from the ceramic bowl. I smashed the mutt over the head violently until he completely ceased to move. This took much longer than I had really expected. This was what made me realize that this simple tool, this plain, round piece of steel was not going to cut it.

I needed something sharp, and I needed it fast. I looked down at the solid cement floor – no pieces to break off, nothing. I keep looking. Cement, everything is cement. I pick the steel nozzle up again and break the ceramic sink into large white pieces onto the floor. The ceramic is too soft. It crumbles in my hand as I try to begin my incision right below the dog's jaw.

Ah ha! I remember the small pocketknife and I become so overwhelmed with joy, I almost jump out of the small cave I've trapped myself in. I take the knife and carefully cut from the bottom of the mutt's jaw to the bottom of his dark brown stomach. As blood oozes all over the cold, cement floor, I realize that I should have taken a different approach. I should have made smaller cuts so that Dante doesn't get lost in a rapid river of blood. I quickly covered the sewer drain to stop all liquid from leaving the building.

Next, I carefully inspected the inside of the dog's mouth. You can never be too careful when it comes to these things. Dante could have been crushed between some teeth, or lodged down in some gums. When I didn't find him there, I moved on to the esophagus. I ripped open the carcass so that the dog's fur laid flat on the ground. From here, I had to cautiously slice this cylindrical tube while I searched through its contents. Still, no Dante. Next was the stomach.

That was when I heard it. Sirens. How the hell am I going to get out of here when it is surrounded by hundreds of people? Cops, citizens, and children. I think to myself, 'Man, I'm really stuck this time.'

Chapter 8

The sirens started off faint. As they got closer, my pulse quickened and my nose twitched. Think! Think! How am I going to get out of here? I gripped the knife harder in my hand as my mind ran over all the possibilities. I couldn't get caught... I would surely go to jail. I know what would happen to a white, fluffy bunny in jail. I could hear the sirens getting closer and closer. It was time to act.

I grabbed the knife and made a deep cut

behind the vermin's throat, severing the esophagus.

Then I pulled at the entrails with all my might. I

heard a wet snap as the stomach detached from the

intestines. I made a few more quick cuts to separate

the rest of the stomach. I bundled the guts into a

nice ball and put them under my arm. I opened the

toilet lid and looked down into the festering pool.

Luckily, it was one of those cheap porta-potty type

toilets that were just a hole in the ground. It was

now or never. I clutched the bloody entrails and

hopped down into the slop. As I jumped, I could

hear the cars screeching to a halt.

PLOP! The brown soup was all around me. I

fought the urge to gag as the horrid smell reached

my nose. I quickly waded over to the side and held

still. It was dark in the hole. I felt around the edges with my free hand. The sides were slick and slimy. I suddenly felt a rather deep depression in the side. It was about half a foot into the side. I crouched down into the waste and moved into the depression. The filth was up to my whiskers. I was about to wretch when I heard the voice come over the loudspeaker.

"Come out!" screamed the rough-sounding man. They were just outside the bathroom door. I fought every urge to stand up and struggle to get out.

"COME OUT! You have five seconds to comply!"

I couldn't hear the countdown. My ears were completely filled with sewage. Suddenly I saw a burst of light as the door was thrust open. I could feel the men move around above me. I stood

perfectly still. A shaft of light pierced the dark void

I was in. Another one joined it, as the police shined

their flashlights down to discover what had

happened to me. I heard muttering and cursing as

they retreated out of the shack. I rose up a little

from my brown covering to hear what was going

on. I heard the sound of the dog being pulled from

the bathroom floor. It sounded like a wet mop

running across concrete.

"Well, the sick bastard isn't in there. He

probably gutted the thing somewhere else and threw

the rest in there. Jesus, there are some damn sick

people in the world. Come on guys; get that nasty

thing outta here!" The rough policeman shouted

some more orders. Gradually, I heard the cars start

up and take off. I waited for what seemed an eternity. When I thought it had been enough time, I came out into the middle of the poo. How am I going to get outta here? The top was about four feet above my head. I took the now brown entrails and put them in between my teeth. I wiped my hands as best I could and made ready to jump. I sprang with all my might and caught a hold of the rim. I struggled to pull myself up. The sewage was sticking to my fur and weighing me down. As it slowly dropped from me, I was able to struggle higher and higher. Finally, I was able to get the rim under my arm. With my last bit of strength, I made it over the rim and slid down to the bloody floor. I laid in the blood for several minutes to catch my breath.

When I had caught my breath, I cautiously opened the door and peered out. It was dark and there was no one around. I carefully crept out and went to some nearby bushes. The way I was covered, I would be noticed immediately. Ah-Ha! The pond was just about fifty feet from here. I took off as fast as I could. I had to get this stuff off of me. The pond shimmered like a silver mirror in the moonlight. I set the entrails on the edge and leapt in. I did my best to wash myself clean of the putrid slop. After about five minutes, I came back to the edge and gathered my prize. I took off as fast as I could toward my house.

I slammed the door behind me as I burst into my house. I walked to my kitchen and put the guts on the counter. I felt around in my pockets for my knife. I must have left it at the bathroom. Oh well. I grabbed the Ginsu and laid the guts flat. I took the knife and slit from end to end. I spread the guts open and looked for the little candy corn. At last I found him, deep inside the stomach. He was filthy with blood and bits of stomach. I took Dante and ran him under some water. I could hear him shout at me from under the water.

"Oh Leonard, thank God you found me! It was so horrible in the belly of that beast."

"I would never let you go, Dante. You mean everything to me. You tell me the word of God. How could I let you go?" I replied. I held Dante very close to me. He felt so good in my paws. I looked down at him with a smile as he lay in my paw. I noticed that my fur was now a dull red. I had better take a bath before it stains.

I started to feel like real rabbit again as I stepped out of the shower. I dried myself off and settled on my couch with a carrot. What was on TV? I flipped over to CNN to catch the news of the day. I caught the end of the national report. I heard the anchor say that local news was up next.

"The Big Apple is getting ready for another Easter. The streets have their banners up and the shops are setting up for the sales. Yes it seems everyone is ready for Easter. And of course the children are going to have fun this year too. The Central Park Easter Egg Hunt is only two days away. The event features a loveable Easter Bunny that hides the eggs for the kids to find." The screen showed a man in a bunny suit performing for kids. It made me sick. "Participation is limited so please sign your kids up at the Tavern on the Green by tomorrow." The news report kept going but I didn't listen to it anymore. I just kept picturing the big, white fake staring at me from the television. He was the Easter Bunny?! I don't even own a pocket watch, let alone wear it! This is what people think the Easter Bunny looks like? This was not only insulting; it was blasphemy. Didn't anyone in this city remember what this damn holiday is about? This egg-hunt has nothing to do with the Lord God. My eggs represent the rebirth of Jesus – the whole point of the holiday. The fake bastard in the suit's eggs represent depravity and commercialization. They weren't even real eggs in his basket. They were little fake ones with candy inside. People had taken a religious idea and commercialized it. They found just one more thing to slap an advertisement on. The little eggs would be chock full of fat-free sin. That gave me an idea. They were hollow...

I took Dante out of my pocket and stared at him, trying to find the answers to my sinister plan. "Is it right? Will it work?" I stammered.

He slowly answered, "Yes. An example must be set." I knew what I had to do.

The next day, bright and early, I hopped in my car and drove. I drove for hours until I couldn't recognize any of the town names. I turned off of Interstate 92 onto a little county highway. The scenery was so much more calming than the chaos of the city. The little houses in neat rows looked so inviting. I felt at home. I stopped at the little gas station in the town. I filled up my Subaru and went in to pay. I forked over the fifteen dollars and asked the attendant where I could get what I wanted. She told me that just outside of town was a little store that could help me. I followed her directions and pulled into this beat-up gun shop. I walked in and looked around. The place had seen better days and probably never seen a dust rag. Everything was arranged in nice, little dusty rows. The place smelled like pizza and must. I walked up to the counter and rang the bell for service.

"Yeah, I'm comin'," said the voice from the back. The man that came to the front was about fifty and needed a shave. He had little smears of red on the sides of his mouth. That explained the pizza smell. He was a grizzled old man. Just the guy I was looking for. "What can I do you for?"

"Hi, I was wondering if you might be able to help me. You wouldn't happen to sell..." I told him what I wanted. Amazingly, he didn't look shocked when I asked. He even was able to help me with the mechanics of it. Honestly, I never have dealt with this kind of stuff before. He didn't ask me why I wanted all of this, just took my money and went back into his little room. I bundled up my purchases and hopped back in my car.

I got back to the city around five. I had one more place to go. I went to the grocery store that was just down the street from my house. I went in and bought a thing of carrots and some plastic Easter eggs. You know, the hollow kind. I drove down the block to my house and parked the car. I brought my things into my house and set them on the table. I pulled the shades and set to work. I filled the eggs and set everything like the old man had told me. I made four eggs. Now all I had to do was wait.

I took Dante out to let him see my gift to the Lord. He reassured me that I was doing God's will. I carefully took my creations and set them near the door. I could hardly wait.

The next day finally came. I had stayed up most of the night thinking about what I had done. I kept picturing the results. How sweet it will be. I took my four beauties and gently set them in my car. The clock on the dash said 7:06. Perfect. I would get there before the crowds started showing up. It was short drive to Central Park. I parked my car and took out my babies. Casually, I walked to the Tavern on the Green. The egg-hunt was to take place just behind it. The area was roped off in preparation. I was early enough that no one was out yet. Hmmm, where to put these pastel pretties?

I put the first one near a bush. I bent down to ready it. I carefully twisted the top of the shell until I saw the little pressure trigger pop out of the hold I made in the shell. I prayed to God that I had put enough explosive in the egg to keep the switched depressed on the ground. Otherwise... Well, I didn't want to think about otherwise. I set the egg down firmly on the pressure switch. I took my hand off and let out a sigh of relief. I set the rest of them and went back to the Tavern. I went inside and sat at a table. Within fifteen minutes, the people had started to show up. I could see through the window the imposter going about in a comical way, setting the eggs on the ground. He was putting on a show for the children. Thankfully, he was done in about ten minutes. My carrot juice and carrot cake arrived just as the gun was shot to signal the beginning of the hunt. I took a sip of my juice. I had just taken a bite from my cake as I heard a loud blast, followed by another one about four seconds later. The screams started. I smiled to myself and took another bite. It never had tasted sweeter.

Chapter 9

Oh, it was beautiful. I watched all the screaming parents running to what was left of their children. It was so hard to wipe away the self-satisfied smirk that crept onto my face as I saw them crying out, grasping scraps of pretty blue Easter dresses with the white lace trim now stained red with blood. I finished the delicious carrot cake and juice and looked around for a recycling bin to put my bottle in. There wasn't one in sight. People these days just don't give two craps about our environment. I looked back over at the chaos I had caused. Two of the adults who looked like they might have set up this little blasphemous display were picking up a few of the remains of a little boy out of a near-by bush. Everyone was hysterical. I only wished I had made more than four. I laughed under my breath. Then all of a sudden I got very paranoid. My eyes darted around the area, scanning for anyone who might have suspected. Any old bunny sitting over in the corner in a Tavern watching an Easter event was not too suspicious, but I looked down at my paws. They were still somewhat stained a brownish orange color. That damn dog. To think I almost lost Dante. Paranoia hit again, and again my eyes darted around. I saw a man on his cell phone. He was surely calling the cops. I reached for my breast pocket, but my attention was diverted elsewhere.

"Oh, God!" I heard someone scream. One of the mothers of the stupid little brats I blew up was freaking out, naturally. She was going crazy, but what can you expect from a woman who just saw her child blown into pieces right in front of her eyes at a community event that was supposed to boost the morale of the town. I expected it, all the screaming, the hysteria, the sobbing. I was actually looking forward to it. But this woman, what she said... Oh, what she said! She kept sobbing, screaming, "Oh God! Jesus! Oh my God! Why? Why did this happen?!" She looked up to the sky, holding her little Johnny, or rather little Johnny's head and torso as that was all that was left in one piece. She looked up to the serene white clouds and she screamed at the top of her lungs, a blood curdling sound that would have yanked the heart of any normal person right out of their sacrilegious chests. "WWHHHYYYYY?!!! Why did you do this, God?!"

That stupid little cooze! How dare she blame Him? I could feel the blood rushing up to my face. It's a good thing I still had some of my winter coat to cover the flush. I started breathing very heavily. That ignorant broad! Why did He do this? I'll tell you why you dumbass little…I started to count to ten, a little anger management trick Dante had taught me. He told me I needed to stop killing at random. He said I was gong to end up slipping up and get caught.

I counted 10...9...8...

It wasn't working. I stroked the shiny pistol in my breast pocket. Oh, how good it would feel, I thought to myself. My finger brushed Dante's tiny body next to the gun. I remembered what he told me. No, I can't.

I counted 7...6...5...

"Do it."

"What?" I asked.

Dante's voice came small and muffled behind the fabric. "Do it. I know what you're thinking. I want you to do it."

I reached into my pocket and pulled him out. "I can't. Remember, you said no more random killing. With all these people here I'm sure to get cau - "

"Shut up. Listen to what I tell you. This stupid woman is blaming God! This type of bull is exactly why we are doing what we are doing. She's here celebrating Easter…BULL! She's celebrating a commercialized holiday signified by candy and a little gift-bearing bunny. She doesn't care that Jesus has washed our sins away with His blood. She doesn't even know what your eggs represent. None of these morons do. They need to be taught a lesson, Leonard. And you are the chosen one. Do it." I stared at him for a second. "Do it," he whispered. I nodded and put his little orange triangular body back in my pocket.

I grabbed my .45 and ran out the Tavern. I ran straight to where the psychotic, screaming woman was. I grabbed her short, shiny blonde hair. She could have been one of those girls out of the Herbal Essence commercials, for sure. I yanked her up from her kneeling position – the position people pray in and here she is at an Easter event and with all her blasphemy, she might as well be beckoning to Satan. I put the cold steel to her temple and heard her take in a short breath through her teeth; sure to be her last, as she closed her eyes and whimpered.

"Anyone so much as twitches and you will all take witness to the making of the newest addition to the Modern Art display that will be featured in the Guggenheim museum. Yes, I'm talking her brains all over this place. Now, do I have

139

your full attention?" Everyone was looking at me with their big doe eyes, deer caught in the headlights. I smiled my sinister smile, keeping my two Crest white buckteeth hidden. "Good," I said.

In the frightened silence of the crowd, I sensed something. My ears twitched. That man on the damn cell phone. Bang. Without even looking, I fired a shot directly to my right and in an instant the gun was back to its spot on the Blaspheme Queen's lovely temple. She let out another little whimper and a general gasp came from the crowd shortly before a loud *thump-thump* was heard. Precision shooting comes in handy in times like this, and I silently thank Dante.

"Now, I want you all to listen very closely. You have all been victimized and yet are all simultaneously guilty of the same crime. What crime you ask? The de-religionization of our nation. Do any of you even know what Easter is a celebration of?"

"I do," called a voice from the crowd.

"Shut up." Bang. Automatically, I fired my hollow point bullet in the direction the voice came from. Bullseye. I looked over just in time to catch a glimpse of a man wearing an all black suit with a white collar just before he fell to the soft ground. *Thump-Thump.* Oops, oh well, I thought. "Any other comments?" I asked. Utter silence, it is golden. "Now, why don't you all just sit down," I said and threw Blondie to the ground. "I'm going to tell you a little story." They complied like the good little sheep they are.

"A long time ago – well 2,037 years to be exact – a child was born to a virgin. A miracle to say the least, but it was only the first of many this man would perform. Well, long story short, he was sent to Earth by God to save all your ignorant asses. In case you still aren't following me, you atheist bastards, I'm talking about Jesus. Yeah, he came here for your salvation, so you all wouldn't rot in Hell like you deserve to. The best thing to come to this planet and what do you humans do? You crucified him. Idiots! But not even that could keep the J-man down. No, sir, not then, and not now." My voice began to raise, "Because we're coming back!"

"Whoa, easy, killer," I heard Dante say to me. "Just stick to the storytelling for now."

I was shaking with anger. I took a deep

breath. "We're coming back," I said a little quieter,

"just like He did 2,004 years ago." I paced around

the crowd, dragging Miss Atheist along, trying to

gain composure. Sometimes, I just get a little too

carried away. That was another thing Dante taught

me to work on: patience. After all, it is a virtue. So I

took a couple minutes to walk around the crowd,

giving each and every worthless piece of human

flesh an evil glare to send the message home. "You

see," I began again, "all you corporate whores, you

have all been brainwashed. You have been weaned

off the milk of the Lord Jesus and have substituted

His love with milk chocolate, beer, and cocaine.

You are Godless. And without God, you are just

meaningless bags of skin and bones. Jesus loves

everyone. Everyone but you, for you are the pieces of His crap. No, what am I saying? His crap is like gold. But you people, you are the turds in the toilet that our world has become. The kind that don't flush, even after the third try. That is what you are – worthless. You have forsaken Him. And if that is not enough, you are teaching it to your children. The innocent ones," I said and pointed to the remaining pieces of little Johnny. I grabbed another chuck of the Queen's hair and tugged, "So, why did this happen, you ask. Because you have forsaken Him. And in turn, you have forsaken your children," I said and turned to the rest of the crowd, "all of you." I paced around again, debating how far I should take this sermon. "Jesus was resurrected 2004 years ago today. And he has been sitting at the right hand of our God, waiting for two millennia to come back. And after all those years of watching you humans turn from Him, watching this holiday that is supposed to celebrate His resurrection and your eternal life through Him being turned into a holiday that celebrates little candy eggs and bunny rabbits that carry baskets, watching America commercialize His holiday, the same way it does everything, ladies and gentlemen, He is pissed! And he has been waiting up there for the day when he is to come back to this earth, this toilet. That day will be Judgement Day. And how do you think he is going to look on to the likes of you? The same way you look at Him. Void of any passion or belief. You will be forsaken. So, being the forgiving God that He is, God has sent me here. He has sent me to teach you all a little lesson before His son loses His heavenly patience." Bang. The Blaspheme Queen's body fell limp to the ground, her beautiful blonde hair now a lovely shade of red with bits of gray matter splattered throughout. I turned to my left where a man was standing wearing a pastel colored Easter egg dappled tie. I shot him right where the biggest egg was. I turned again to see an old woman wearing a pair of Easter egg earrings. I shot them both right off her ears, just nicking the earlobe to spray a little bit of blood. I turned one last time. I saw another older lady crouched down by her husband, the priest I had shot. She was the only one wearing a cross, and the only one whose eyes met mine without any fear in them. I decided to spare her life. Bang.

* * *

The next thing I remember, I was driving down some foreign road in my Subaru. The windshield wiper blades were going almost full speed. It looked like a typical rainy spring day. The sky was a gray color, not too light because of the ominous rain clouds, not too dark because the sun was lingering somewhere beyond them. Days like this usually make me feel tranquil and almost happy, but not on this trip. I felt queer. It was like I was in a trance, under a spell, or something. I didn't know where I was driving to, but I most definitely had a destination. Something was calling to me, drawing me to it. I didn't have a clue what it was. I just knew I had to get to this place and had to get there as soon as possible. I threw the short throw shifter into second, put the gas pedal down as far as it could go, popped the clutch, and listened to my Yokohoma all-weather racing tires squeal against the pavement while I felt the turbo-charged 6-cylinder engine throw me back against my seat. The rain beat even harder against the windshield. It was getting difficult to see where I was going. That didn't matter though, I was driving by instincts and pure unrefined adrenaline. I took a left. Then I swung a right. Right here, I knew. I slammed on the brakes instantly. I hopped out of the car, right into a giant mud puddle. I didn't care. Frantically, I looked around. Where was it? Jesus, I didn't even know what I was looking for. Straight ahead of me, my instincts yelled. I ran full speed about fifty yards. There, in the middle of a grassy meadow near some railroad tracks laid a little tiny bunny rabbit. Dead. All bloody and limp. This is what I was searching for. This little bunny drew me here. How and why, I may never know. I sat down right next to it in the mud and the rain, and I wept.

Faintly in the distance, I heard the cling-clinging of keys. Buzzzzzzzz-Clunk-kachuck-bang-chink. Awake. 'What the hell was that? Where am I?' I thought. I felt a jabbing pain in my ribs with a warm gooey feeling accompanying it as I looked around. Concrete walls surrounded me, eight feet by eight feet. I realized I was lying on an uncomfortable bed that didn't even have a mattress. Where was my SleepNumber bed? I sat straight up. Bars. 'Oh my God! Dante help! I'm in a cage.'

Chapter 10

I stared around at my enclosure. The cold
steel bars made me shiver as I thought of the
impending doom that was awaiting me. I continued
my surveillance and noticed a single window cut
into the distant concrete wall on the opposite side of
the cell. The window itself had bars blocking it that
were identical to those impeding my progress
toward escape. Lying on the stone floor, underneath
the small, yet barred window, was an old worn out

mattress that had obviously been the resting place for more than a couple of previous pathetic captives. From where I was lying on the freezing stone floor, I could see many dark-colored spots upon the mattress where the inhabitants had apparently been unable to either control themselves or had simply not made it to the tiny silver bucket resting in the corner.

Suddenly, I felt another sharp jabbing pain in my side. It felt so horrible, I almost screamed out in anguish. Instead, I chose to bite my lip and screw my face up in pain so I probably wound up looking something close to Quasimodo out of Victor Hugo's The Hunchback of Notre Dame or something fairly similar. At least I remained silent. After the pain began to subside, I looked down at my torso only to see a poor attempt at a patch-up job. The gauze that

was wrapped around the gaping hole in my flesh

was already soaked a deep crimson color all the

way through. Besides this obvious oversight in my

medical treatment, the tape holding the gauze on my

dirty white fur, now sticky with perspiration, was

slowly peeling and falling away. Being the

perfectionist I am, I tried, in vain, to reattach the

adhesive. As I was trying to replace the sorry

excuse for a bandage, I noticed the warden sitting

about twenty feet away. He seemed to be a

relatively short man, not too tall anyway. He was a

little on the heavy side, probably from eating a few

too many Krispy Kremes or Dunkin Donuts while

on duty. I don't think I have ever seen a single

officer of the law that actually looked like he had

taken care of himself. They all looked like they had

gone too heavy on this or that and just "didn't have

time" to work off the needless excess calories they

had ignorantly consumed. Come to think of it, he

had probably been consuming tons of little

chocolate eggs of sin or evil poultry-shaped

marshmallow confections before he had been called

to actually do his job for once. As I continued to sit

on the floor and clutch my side, he kept staring

straight at me, as if he were trying to see right into

my very thoughts. Apparently he had been told to

keep a close watch over me. Could you blame him

or his superiors? I had already proven myself a

maniac. I could face the facts. After all, I had

mercilessly killed Mr. Snyder at the rest area, Mrs.

Snyder in her twelfth-floor hospital room, a dog in a

park facility, and many innocent people that morning at the sacrilegious display of gluttony, greed, and immorality. At this point, I wouldn't even trust myself!

So I just sat silently on the cold stone floor awaiting the upcoming conversation. I stared at the warden, and he stared right back. I could tell it wasn't going to be very pleasant, to say the least. I sat in my spot and pondered about how witty I would be when he would inevitably reproach me for all my actions. He would refuse to listen, and I would continue to educate him on why what I had done was nothing immoral. No, it had actually been to save those pathetic little sacrilegious idiots' souls. I would make him understand. However long it would take, I knew that I had to make him see the irrefutable reason behind all these previous

transgressions of mine.

Finally, the warden stopped surveying me

and decided to break the silence. "You sick SOB,"

he snarled. "You should be thankful that you're

behind those bars. Plenty of infuriated New Yorkers

are standing right outside wanting to decide your

fate for themselves. Personally, I want to hand you

over to them."

"Then why don't you?" I calmly inquired.

Internally, I felt horrible due to the hole in my side

that continued to cause me to convulse with pain

and also because of my nagging conscience. Neither

would concede to leave me alone. At this point, I

was struggling for any connection between myself

and reality. So I continued to stare at the pudgy man

and try my hardest to make polite conversation. In light of my situation, I think I was handling myself pretty well.

"The police chief wants this to be a lawful decision," he grunted. "As long as you die, I don't really care how you're tried." Well, at least he was being honest with me. Most people would lie and say something either partially polite or simply start ripping into you, but he just stated his opinion and continued to watch my every movement.

"Do you even realize the significance of all I've done?" I asked, searching for some type of interaction with this stubborn jailor. I figured, if not for some type of enlightenment for one of us, the conversation would pass some of the unpleasant time I was to spend locked up. Plus, he kind of

157

intrigued me. H might make a good student. All he needed was to be molded by my capable hands. Hey, even old dogs can learn new tricks. While he might have been slightly more than just old, he could prove an interesting subject to study and try to reason with.

"Face it, you ain't got a chance." It was apparent that he was tired of taking the effort to talk to me. So, he chuckled to himself, turned away from me, and walked down the corridor. He probably was on a sugar low and needed to go saturate his arteries with wholesome saturated fats. As if he needed any. Besides, he had obviously forgotten about his not-so-little order to watch over me. Left alone, I finally relaxed into a calmer state right below paranoia.

As I sat alone in the cell, I started replaying all the events that had occupied my life for the last several days. They were like slides running through a mini-projector in my head. Pictures of reddish-gray matter staining the back of an open bathroom stall, a frail woman's body flying through the air while convulsing with electricity, and a blonde woman holding a young child's mutilated body in her arms, kept flooding my thoughts. Insanity wasn't even an option to plead at my trial. I obviously knew what I was doing. Otherwise, my point would have been made with fewer bodies. However, I had to figure out something to bargain with.

A thought suddenly struck me. Where was Dante? I started searching myself. I guess my concern for the injury along with the worries accompanying my near future had totally overshadowed any thoughts of the Great Almighty One. As I came to my senses, I continued to search for the mastermind behind all I had accomplished. Without him, I was just a cute fluffy white bunny rabbit with a strong sense of justice. I had no means of following through with any of my solutions. Simply put: I needed Dante to help me succeed.

Let's see. He wasn't resting in my pocket where I had left him. Luckily, while imprisoning me, they had not decided to take my clothes in exchange for an orange striped jumpsuit. He wasn't underneath me. Where was he? Where would a single stale candy corn go to in such a situation? Just then I noticed a small speck of dusty orange lying next to the putrid mattress on the floor under the window. I painfully crawled over to it and saw Dante lying there. I slowly breathed a sigh of relief.

"Dante, are you alright?" I feebly asked as I picked the small piece of candy up and pulled him to my chest. It hurt so bad to breathe, let alone talk.

"Yes, I'm here. Calm down," he responded. It was amazing how well he was controlling his emotions. I was openly worried while he barely moved a muscle. Funny, he was always calm, except when he told me to execute innocent people in front of the masses.

"We're in jail!"

"Thank you, Captain Obvious." Well, at least he still had a sense of humor, even when I was panicking right in front of him.

"How're we supposed to complete our ultimate mission if we're stuck behind bars?" I know I sounded hysterical, but I couldn't help myself. After all, it's always the cute ones that can't make it in jail. At this point, I didn't think I had another option other than five-to-twenty in a state prison or penitentiary. "Come on Dante. You've always saved me before. You can't let me down now. How's it gonna happen this time?"

"Leonard," he slowly muttered. He didn't sound too hopeful this time. It kinda worried me. "You've finally gotten yourself into something I don't have a cure for." Then he was silent. I sat and stared at him astonished that after all he had put me through, he was the one that was giving up. I had obeyed his orders, found him in the stomach of an overweight mutt's innards, even tried to control myself until he told me to "do it", and yet now he was giving up on me. Seems appropriate, doesn't it? I did all the work and he didn't want to take even part of the responsibility. Apparently, it was his way to take me up out of my hopeless dependence for aid. I knew I was on my own. I laid Dante next to one giant yellow stain on the mattress. I knew he wouldn't help me any longer. I took one last look at the little stale candy corn, covered with dirt, dust, and grime and thought about what I needed to do.

I sat next to the pathetic sleeping arrangements, stained with urine and other body juices, and tried to think of some type of a solution. Nothing came immediately to me. I looked around the cell: over at the bars still standing impressively and blocking any hope of an exit, at the bucket in the corner that was now partially full due to that carrot juice I had drank earlier, over at the festering mattress where my mentor still lay silent as a stone. Then, I looked up and noticed that the sunlight that had previously filled my cell with warmth and light was now retreating through the grate cover across the window. Dusk was swiftly approaching along with the ever encroaching twilight. There was nothing inside to capture my attention, so I pulled my heavy, sweat-stained body up to the window. It was just high enough above my current spot to make me stretch my body just to reach the windowsill. The gauze and tape pulled painfully tight against my fur, trying vainly to impede my movements. However, I had been crouching on the rock-hard floor so long already that any movement, either slight or immense, put an incredible strain on the muscles involved. So I winced through my discomfort and stared out at the city surrounding me.

Looking to the right, I saw a few advertisements for candy and other products aimed toward unsuspecting consumers. I couldn't believe it. Even with my deeply meaningful demonstration, people still refused to acknowledge their own faults and inconsistencies towards faith. The human race frankly disgusts me. It's almost as if they revel in their ignorance. As I continued my search, I found, to my utter surprise, a single symbol of the true meaning of Easter revealed right in front of the gorgeous sunset.

A chapel down the street had a crucifix upon the steeple draped in a white piece of cloth. Now that was the true significance to this newly commercialized holiday. Suddenly, an idea came to me. I realized how much my mission truly meant. The J-man had been tortured and sentenced to death by those that did not understand him. I seemed to be in a similar, yet not-so-gruesome predicament. Nobody was listening to me, even though I was willing to try to give them some type of personal salvation. As with the J-man, however, they refused to listen to me either. If only I could bring all of his sacrifices of two centuries ago into the foreground of the people's minds. Nowadays, their brains are so full of mush that nothing worthwhile really had a chance to ever stick in that mess of worthless gray matter they consider to be so important. I had to remind them about what the holiday was supposed to mean. Obviously, my rampage had not even made a dent in their ignorance or else they had simply pounded it back out. There had to be another way to make them see how much things needed to change. Other than shooting them down in public, I mean. If I could just keep my emotions, especially anger, under control, I knew I was the one to make them see their human fallacies. So I sat there at the window and prepared myself for what was to come.

Chapter 11

The evening ahead seemed as if it would be to unpleasant for this rabbit to bear. I would have no more with Dante, as he had given up on me and the crusade. I myself had not completely given up, but was losing the hope that drove me. As the daylight waned a light shone on the cross that headed the church down the road. The cross stood like a beacon of hope for a boat in a perfect storm.

I spent a couple of mindless hours staring

out the window. When I fell from the trance of the

last few hours I realized it was now dark, well as

dark as it could be in a busy nightlife city. I realized

that I had to do something. I had yet to complete my

goal of opening the eyes of those mindless pigs that

had inherited the earth. I felt that I owed it to the J-

Man to complete my crusade. I began to brainstorm.

I thought, 'How does one get out of a maximum

security prison, where one is being watched at all

times by an armed guard?' The thought made me

feel hopeless, but I knew I would be able to figure

something out even without that no good, worthless,

little shit of a candy corn. I began to forsake Dante

for not helping me in my greatest time of need. I

had no luck with ideas and became quite upset. I

began to think about the good ole days of when life was normal and I had yet to kill anyone. I thought of watching my crappy, little nineteen inch Apex television and falling asleep in my superbly comfortable Sealy Posturepedic bed. Then, all of a sudden, it hit me. I had thought of my way out of this prison, this cage, this trap. I had spent many lonely hours watching The Hunting Channel to see if any of my relatives had been caught or shot. I once saw an episode of small game hunting where they set a trap and came back the next day to only find the foot of a rabbit, a good friend of mine actually. My escape would be similar in that I would gnaw off my paw. I would gnaw off my paw forcing them to put me in the sick ward of the prison, which has much less security. From the sick ward I could make an escape.

I laid down that night squirming with anticipation of the day to come. Laying there I thought of which paw I would gnaw off tomorrow. It was a hard decision, but I ultimately decided to lose my left and keep my right. At this point I was so happy I forgot about my anger towards Dante and told him of my plan.

"Dante, Dante," I whispered careful not to wake the guard, "I have come up with a plan for our escape."

"What is your plan that brings you so much whispering excitement," he whispered. I told him of my plan to gain access to the sick ward. He was quite excited, and said, "Leonard, I knew I had taught you well. Now, all you must do is get us to that sick ward, and I will handle the rest from there."

This time I gathered much faith in my small candy friend. I knew that Dante could pull me through the rest of our escape. I began to get thoughts of what I would do when I escaped. I let these thoughts ferment in my brain as I slowly slipped into the nightly trance known as sleep.

I awoke the next morning to the yells and calls of the baboons in the cells next to me. They were nothing but a bunch of barbaric imbeciles. Each of them here, waiting on death row, where I had been oddly placed. I had yet to have a trial and was already being treated as though I had a first class ticket to meet my maker. I guess I understood though; I knew that a trial against me would result in such actions. This is why my plan would have to work. I decided the plan would happen this very evening for sure, no questions asked. I spent most of the day listening to the conversations of the unclean prisoners that surrounded my crap-ass cage. One man spoke to his inmate saying, "I had it all planned out, my whole life. Now, I'm stuck here. I had dreams to have a family with her, and get a real job rather than working at Texas Road House as a busboy. She had to have known that it was going to be beautiful," the man took a breath, "but things didn't all work out, as you can tell. I came home to the trailer behind my grandma's house that I lived in to find that slut sleeping with my best friend. I was so torn with anger at the sight of it that I ran over to my bed and grabbed my gun. I took that silver

mechanism of my hate and planted two in that slut's

stupid face. The shots flew through her skull

shooting her brains all over my friend, who had an

orgasm just as the bullets ripped through. Next, I

turned to my friend and shot him 28 times in the

chest and face totally destroying my bed and his

body," another pause came, then he spoke again

saying, "And that's why I'm here." This man's story

sickened me, but also gave me a feeling of good

doing for the same revenge I had been bringing

down upon those sinning against God.

The guard had apparently been listening to

the same story as I because he quickly stood up with

a green face. His fat ass was not speedy enough to

take him to the trash can, and I saw the day's worth

of Twinkies flood the floor in liquid form. He puked violently. It was almost so painful it hurt me watching, but I enjoyed it deeply. The puke continued to flow from his oral orifice, spraying the ground yellow and white. Then, the puke came so hard blood began to flow, and his face changed colors. He fell onto his back with blood and puke spewing out his mouth like Old Faithful in Yellowstone. He was most certainly choking now, and had little chance at living without someone helping him. No one was around to help the guard, and he consequently died, choking on his own puke and blood.

The dead guard laid there for almost an hour before the next man came on for his shift and saw him lying there. The new shift guard screamed out in terror at what he saw when he walked into the corridor. He ran quickly over to his fellow guard. He then called for an ambulance and more help on his walkie-talkie, but what little good this would do as everyone knew the man was dead. They should have brought in a hearse instead of an ambulance, but sure enough an ambulance and the coroner came. The coroner pronounced the man dead on the spot. The morgue mobile came in, and took the guard away.

A still quietness fell over all the prisoners until lunch came to us. The food was like a talking catalyst, bringing back conversation between the many rowdy prisoners of my corridor. I received my lunch last, and was horrified to see that we were given government cheese and rabbit sandwiches. I was unable to eat such a disgracing meal, and decided to go without food for this afternoon. I sat back on my bed, and began more observations of my fellow prisoners.

There was a man about three or four cells down that had got done eating, and appeared to be alone in his cell. He began to yell at the prisoner across from him, and then I heard laughing from the cell across from him as well as choking sounds. The guard ran down to the man's cell to see what was going on, and yelled, "What the hell is going on down there?" When he got there, seeing the man imitating the dead guard choking, he became infuriated. He told the man in the cell to put his hands through for handcuffing. The prisoner did as he was told, laughing. The guard put the cuffs on the man, then opened the door. He pulled the prisoner out into the corridor for all of us to see. He said, "Okay, you sick bastard you. You ready for some real fun?" With that, the guard pulled out his club and began laying into the prisoner. He beat the man repeatedly in the back, over and over. The prisoner cried so loud for him to stop, but there was no stopping the pissed off guard. He then did something that even sickened me – he began beating the man's face in. With each hit to the face, the club became more and more bloody. The blood flew back off the club and onto the other cells when he brought it up to swing down again. He kept beating the man's face in, then the man's eye popped out and rolled across the ground. This did not faze the guard as he continued beating this man in the face. It was disturbing to see the blood flowing on the ground and off the club. The next hit was the hit that broke the pumpkin. He swung with such force it blew the man's skull apart. Little pieces of my favorite gray matter flew all over, as did skull fragments and blood, but not even this stopped the deranged guard as he beat the busted pumpkin into a flat piece of gelatinous mush on the ground. He then stopped and said, "Let this be a message to all of you: There will be no more screwin' around."

This killed the majority of conversation for the afternoon. I had mostly nervous thoughts flowing through my brain, so I was beginning to become fidgety. Dante spoke words of confidence from my pocket, telling me that I would make it and that we were going to be free. I had to believe him.

He was all I had left in the world, my best friend since bunnyhood.

I got up and began to peer out the window once again. The cross stood there still building my confidence up for the deed I would have to follow through with this evening. I began thinking deeply when my thoughts were broken up by a yell. "Hey! If they would let me, I would do to you what I did to that damn jackass."

I replied, "Why don't you, then?"

"I can't. Everyone wants to see your sick ass fry on the electric chair, and it will happen too. Don't think it won't."

"We will see," I replied with a devilish grin.

"Yes, I will see you frying. Maybe they will forget to wet the sponge. You know what happens when they don't wet the sponge?" he asked with conviction. "I will tell you what happens. You don't get a good hook-up, and you have to be held under longer. All the heat begins to churn and causes you to light on fire, so that you're burning alive. Your skin become black and your hair, phew. Let's just say, it smells horrific," he said. Then, he let out a little chuckle and turned away.

The night finally rolled around, and everyone was asleep. It was time to do that deed that would cause me more pain than anything I had ever felt. I prepared myself for the pain and bit into my arm. It was excruciating pain, but it was a small cost for my freedom. I gnawed away the skin, shooting the blood all over the place and in my mouth. I spit out bits of skin and fur as I went.

Then, I began to rip into the muscle, which was like stripping the meat from a chicken leg. The blood continued to flow like a snowball avalanching down a mountain. The pain built in the same way as the blood. Next was the difficult task of gnawing through the bone. I used my wonderful rabbit teeth to gnaw through the bone like a champion rodent. The pain was horrific, but I suffered through until it was completed. I finally gnawed completely through my arm, and threw it at the sleeping guard. He looked down at what he was holding and screamed out in horror. Then, everything went black.

I woke up the next morning in the sick ward, but with only a gown on. Where were my clothes? Worst of all, where was Dante?

Chapter 12

"Sleeping Fruity has awoken."

"Sue, I told you to cut the cracks. Gimme that shot."

I was very groggy. Probably because of the pain, I must have passed out. Two women were standing over me. One was holding both my arms down, but it didn't feel as if I could have raised them if I wanted to. The other was sticking a needle into my right arm. Both had white coats on, like doctors or workers at LensCrafters.

"I don't know what you think you're doing but you'll–"

–Pay for this, was what I was going to say, but they must have knocked me out. A thick black blanket was pulled over my whole body. And then I slept for a while.

"Lenora."

I realized that I had been kind of awake for a while, but it was like I wasn't really seeing anything or had any thoughts until I heard that voice.

"Lenora." My eyes racked into focus and I saw Dan Ackroyd standing in front of me with one of those white coats on. He held a clipboard in his hand. I assumed he wanted to negotiate with me so that he could play me in some stupid movie of the week or something. But what was this 'Lenora' business?

Dan smiled a little – well, smirked really – and said, "Lenora, I'm Dr. Michelson and I'm going to help you out."

"Listen up, Elwood, I'm the one on a mission from God this time and your little practical joke – or whatever this crap is – is not going to stop me. You're not going to confuse me into signing over the rights of my life for some corporate propaganda to demonize me. We aren't through yet. We *will* be victorious and shine the light of God onto all of you sinners. You cannot silence a prophet!"

That's what I was going to say, but I found that I couldn't speak. Maybe they had cut out my tongue, the crafty devils. But it felt like it was still in there, a little thick and numb, though. Ackroyd merely smiled down at me, the sadist. He then continued to speak and I continued to try to interrupt him and cut off his lies, but they had damaged me so that I couldn't even make a grunt.

"Lenora, I'm going to be frank with you. Your episodes have progressed to a degree that you are a danger to yourself. Dr. Franks believed that you were functional in society and said that you should be emancipated rather than be made a ward of the state or placed in an institution since your aunt's incarceration has made it impossible for *her* to be your legal guardian. But obviously, he was

188

wrong. And since your Aunt Dee shot an abortion

doctor, you will, quite frankly, not be seeing her for

a while. In the month since her arrest, you've

harassed a Wal-mart employee and the staff of St.

Jude's, as well as a patient there. The lobby staff of

TNMTASS aren't complaining of harassment,

luckily for you. They just thought that it was cute

and fun seasonal entertainment for a woman in an

Easter bunny suit to be giving them coffee and

donuts in the morning. Who *is* complaining,

however, is the owner of the dog you've molested in

a public toilet before you proceeded to smear feces

on yourself from one of the toilet bowls. This

incident would have been enough to have you taken

in for observation, if it hadn't been for Dr. Franks'

admission that he had given you the wrong dosage of medication.

"The thing in the park is beyond the pale, though. The authorities in this town don't crack down on public nuisances and they consider loud public proselytizing simply a matter of free speech. But when you add death threats and start spraying people with Tabasco sauce from a squirt gun, you're crossing the line. One little boy got it in his eye. Did you know that? He may have permanent damage to his sight."

I couldn't believe these lies. Some Hollywood scriptwriter sure had been creative to take my holy deeds and spin them into this madness. The attempt to emasculate me by calling me Lenora was the kind of detail only a really talented craftsman would have come up with. And Ackroyd's delivery could have won him an Oscar. So, I spit in his face. It was kind of a feeble spit, nothing too thick about it, but I think it did the trick. He turned around and walked out.

In my mind, I screamed for Dante. Sometimes that has worked when I didn't want to draw attention to myself in public. I could get him to come just by thinking about it forcefully. That's how connected we are.

But this time he didn't come.

I began to panic that they'd done something with him: crushed him, flushed him down a drain, dissected him, *ate* him, or in some other unimaginable way made him a martyr. Without Dante's guidance, I knew I was useless. Oh, I've kidded myself that I could carry on God's will without him, but with Dante gone, I was about as useless as Matthew, Luke, John, Paul, or any of the others without good ole J.C.

My arm had been amputated now, taking off more than just my hand. I'm sure there was some medical excuse to cover up for their sick torture. I was sure that they had paralyzed me, as well. I couldn't move anything below my neck. Next thing they'll do, if I don't sign that release so that they can make fun of me on TV, is they'll get that one guard to bash my head in. Then they'll take my dead, limp hand and make my corpse sign it. And after how I had treated Dante the night before, I would deserve it.

I was a failure. I wept.

"Lenora."

It felt like I had been alone in that hospitaly room for days, but without a clock or window, I had no way of accurately judging the passing of time. Dan Ackroyd was back, with one of the two women who'd given me the shot earlier. She had a wounded, pitying expression on her face. Ackroyd was nearly expressionless.

"Lenora, you won't be seeing Dr. Franks anymore. I don't know how you feel about this, but you definitely won't be seeing him anymore. Franks has been disbarred from practicing because of what he's done with you. After reading his confession, I'm not entirely sure you're even going to understand what I'm talking about. He's taken

advantage of you in innumerable ways."

Let me tell you, I thought this was the

strangest attempt at brainwashing I'd ever heard of.

They get Dan Ackroyd to play a doctor and make

up this whole phony case history about me, even

making me a WOMAN for goodness sake, and then

they expect me to believe it. Like I wouldn't

recognize Dan Ackroyd. Sure, his career hasn't been

that great lately, but he's not exactly an unknown.

Ackroyd went on to tell me that my name

was Lenora, I was a thirty-nine year old woman

who had been a patient of a Dr. Louis Franks for

four years, ever since my 'traumatic divorce'. He

was a psychologist. He had only very recently

admitted to making me totally dependent on him

through a combination of psychological suggestion and drugs. Because he was obsessed with me, Ackroyd said. He went on to go into really vile, unholy detail about this Dr. Franks' perversions and how he used me to fulfill his sick fantasies. I won't go into it, but Ackroyd said it involved bunny costumes. Franks, apparently, was worried that I was "getting out of his grip" because I started to lapse into brief spells of catatonia. I had been living with my aunt, who Franks was able to mollycoddle by assuring her that my treatment regimen was in keeping with God's will. My aunt was supposedly an upstanding Christian who took the matter of the degradation of the world into her own hands. Or, as Ackroyd quaintly put it, a "crazed, extremist zealot, a real Bible-thumping nutcase." With my aunt "getting the wool pulled over her eyes", Franks completely had his way with me. When my aunt was arrested for sending an abortionist speedily to Hell, Franks panicked that I would be put in an institution where I would get 'real help' and he would be exposed. Se he risked doctoring reports, which obviously he'd been doing all along to cover up for his perversities, to make it look like I could 'make it out there in the big world on my own'.

And then I started doing things like shooting people with Tabasco sauce.

And some people have the gall to say that the Bible is far-fetched.

But I have to give them credit. If they really wanted to screw with my head, they sure did their research. Ackroyd gave me some bull that this may all seem surprising to me because I may have suppressed my memories. He then said he was going to show me a photo of Dr. Franks. You won't believe who it was. It was the guy in the rest stop toilet. You know, the one I shot. Well, I mean I think I shot him. Sometimes I'm not so sure about these things.

I must have had quite a look on my face, because Ackroyd then turned to that woman and quietly, but not so quietly that I didn't hear, said, "I think we're getting through. She at least recognizes Franks. It may be time to let her talk. Give her the shot. She'll sleep for a few hours and then be back in control of her body. If she's not ready, we can always freeze her up again and try later."

So the woman, who started to resemble Jane Seymour, stuck a needle in my arm, the one that I had left. And as she did this, through some demon magic, I saw my remaining arm begin to disappear, leaving me looking like Venus de Milo. Except as a guy, of course.

I was again asleep. I don't think I dreamed. I don't think I ever do, actually. But what happened next would probably be mistaken for a dream. But I knew it was real with all the certainty in my soul. There was a new presence in the room.

The J-man. The son. The savior. Mr. Christ.

"Leonard, my child," he said, in a voice as delicate and rich as a fine chocolate treat (NOT a cheap pastel-candy-coated Easter kind), "they have not won. Heaven will yet be victorious. The powers of sin and corruption are strong, but I am here to help. You are the chosen, Leonard. You have not failed. Now with my direct guidance, eternal glory will shine on your brow and you will soon sit next to our Father in the throneroom of the Kingdom."

Tears of joy cascaded all over my broadly smiling face.

"You don't mind if I have a little snack, do you?" Jesus asked.

I shook my head, no of course not. And He reached behind my ear. He kept His fist closed until it was brought back right next to His head. He slowly opened His hand to reveal Dante resting in His palm.

"We won't be needing him anymore, now will we?" And our savior ate Dante. A strange sense of freedom and warmth rushed through my body as His majestic jowls masticated.

Jesus sat next to me on the bed and looked down at where my arms should have been. And, praise be, he brought my arms back, even my hand that I had chewed off.

"You'll be needing those, I think." I noticed that the pain in my side was now gone as well. I had kind of forgotten about it what with the chewing off my hand and all, but now it felt so good that I remembered the severe pain I had had there. "I don't mean to be greedy," Jesus joked, "but I like to be the one with the stigmata, thank you very much."

Wow, Jesus was so cool.

He put His hand on my shoulder and looked very tenderly into my eyes.

"Now, Leonard, here's what you have to do..."

Chapter 13

After Jesus had finished talking and left me,

I took a deep breath. I was excited to finally talk to

the J-man. He was so calm and collected. I couldn't

believe he had chosen me, out of all of his

followers; he had chosen me to talk to. I was

nothing more than a mere rabbit.

He had given me the ultimate task, but

before I could implement his grand plan for me, I

had to escape this dump. I saw some clothes folded

on a chair and decided that it would be a good idea

if I were to wear some human clothes for a while. I

didn't want to bring too much attention to myself.

After I had got dressed, it was time to leave. So I

carefully went to the door and cracked it open. The

coast was clear so I darted for the directory down

the hall to find out where I was. It said that I was on

the 6th floor. I had to carefully plan my route as to

not get caught. I immediately counted out the

possibilities of using the elevators.

I looked around anxiously, fearing capture

every second. Jesus had told me that it would be a

piece of cake to get out of here. I took another look

around, then out of the corner of my eye I saw a

sign on the wall saying "staircase" and I took that as

my chance to escape. I burst through the door and

started my descent. Down and down I went. Finally I reached the bottom and the exit. That's when it all seemed for nothing.

"I have a bad feeling about this," I said to myself. "Alarm will sound when opened." My escape plan was ruined. Ha, so much for planning every step carefully. I told myself that I had to make it out regardless of alarms. I had to make it out of this prison no matter what the consequences may be. I decided I would go for it. I didn't care if the alarm sounded. I was a rabbit – I could outrun any of them without breaking a sweat. I stopped for a moment to kneel and I prayed that I would make it out quickly enough and not get caught. After I finished my prayer I got back up and readied myself for the mad dash out of this place.

I opened the door and started running immediately. I ran right into an empty alley, and noticed that there was no alarm coming from behind so I stopped. The J-man was right; it was a piece of cake to get out. I couldn't believe that I was afraid of a small alarm. It didn't matter now, though. I had acquired freedom and was now able to begin the execution of Jesus' Grand Plan.

I started to walk down the crowded alley. It had been a while since I had been privy to such silence. I was quite refreshing to know that there were places in the world that weren't all about loud noises and rushing. Then I heard Jesus' words, "Leonard, do not waste any time. You must complete the task which I have given you." I nodded to myself and picked up the pace of my walking.

First, I needed to find a gun. Without it, it would be impossible to get anyone's attention. People don't listen to rationality; they only pay attention to those that may threaten their way of life. That's one thing that I've noticed about this poor excuse of a species. Any sort of change will cause them to throw a tantrum and they will do their hardest to make sure that it goes back to the way it used to be. Humans fear change. Only when it's been forced upon them over a period of time do they begin to accept the change.

I exited the alley and looked around the street to see if there were any stores where I could acquire a gun. All I saw were a few clothes shops, a music store, a pawn shop, and a bar and grill. I

quietly called for Jesus and asked him to show me

the way. "The light will never lead you astray," he

replied. I looked up and saw clouds, but there

seemed to be a path just between clouds. I looked to

the ground and saw a path that was lit for me. I

thanked Jesus once again and followed the path.

The path lead me straight into the pawn shop. I

walked in and went to the counter. This grizzled old

man was behind the counter and looked as if he

hadn't cleaned himself in over a week.

"Can I help you?" The man asked.

"I'm looking for a gun," I replied to him.

"Back of the store. Whole rack full of 'em,"

the slob answered. I turned and went to the back of

the store. I saw a lot of antique guns and a few

newer firearms. I found a nine millimeter handgun and grabbed it.

"Do you have any ammo?" I yelled to the front.

"No, just the guns," he yelled back. Damn. Just the gun wasn't enough. I had to think quickly. What was a bunny to do? I decided that I would just have to take the gun and find ammo elsewhere. I reached down for my wallet but it wasn't there. That bastard Ackroyd must have taken it while I was sleeping. He must really be hurting for money. I decided I would just have to make a run for it with the pistol.

I walked up to the front of the store and told the man I needed a phonebook. He turned around and I ran out of the store. I ran a few blocks, then stopped. I looked around and figured the coast was clear. There was nothing on this street that I could use either, just more bars and clothes shops. I had to get ammunition. I remembered that last time I bought the ammunition it was at one of those super-stores. It also wasn't too far from my current position. I started jogging to where I needed to go.

It took only about ten minutes of jogging to get to the store. I entered the building, concealing my weapon beneath my shirt and tucked into my pants. I walked around and asked one of the employees where I could find sporting goods. I followed his directions, laughing as I walked away from the man. I couldn't believe how easy it had been. After the difficulties of killing all those other people, this was a piece of cake.

I reached sporting goods and looked for the guns. There were no employees around, which was probably for the better. I found the gun racks and saw the bullets on a nearby shelf. I picked up a few boxes of the types of bullets I needed. I pulled out the pistol I had and loaded it. I readied the firearm, took off the safety, and started to exit the store.

When I reached the front door, the employee who told me where to look asked if I found everything I needed. I told him that he was a great help and I would definitely be back. I turned and walked out of the store. I left with a grin. I had a fully loaded gun and plenty of extra ammunition in my pockets.

"Leonard! You must finish the task which I have given you," Jesus' voice boomed.

I fell to the ground and answered, "Yes Lord, I shall complete it quickly." I got up and hurried off without thinking of where I was hurrying to. After a few minutes of walking, the answer dawned on me. I should go to the park. I certainly had enough cops around there earlier; it should be no problem to get their attention again.

I started for the park and on my way I laid the plan out in my head. Sure, it may have seemed useless to plan since none of my other plans have gone accordingly, but I felt different about this one. All I had to do was get their attention. That shouldn't be too hard. I was smirking the whole way there.

I arrived at the park sometime in the afternoon. It had already been quite a day – quite a week at that – but it was just about to pay off. I could taste the fruits of victory already and boy, was it sweet.

There were plenty of people at the park when I arrived, most having picnics. The adults were all gathered in groups talking while the children were playing around, running in every which way. One of the kids ran by me coming from the bathroom that I had tried to rescue Dante from.

Thinking back, I was glad Dante was gone. He never really helped me. All he ever accomplished was getting me into situations that I had a difficult time getting out of. He was never very nice about it, either. Always yelling at me to do this and go do that; he was one thankless piece of candy corn. "LEONARD! Now is your chance.

Stop dawdling," Jesus yelled. Once again I nodded,

collecting my thoughts.

I decided it was now or never. I had to grab

one of these children to get the attention of

everyone else. One kid looked like he was about to

go to the bathroom as he suddenly walked by me,

smiling. I took out my gun, picked up the kid, and

pressed the pistol right to his head.

"Nobody move or this kid's brain becomes

dog food!" I yelled. It didn't seem as if anyone

heard me, so I shot into the air which caused

everyone to scream and look my way. "No one

move or this kid is going to die." The people around

me were screaming, and the children were crying.

"Shut those kids up. Shut them up now or I kill all

of you."

The kids stopped crying, the parents stopped screaming, and all of a sudden I felt warm water hit my leg. I looked down and saw the kid I grabbed had peed himself and it was getting all over me. I was suddenly so filled with rage and barked out, "Who are the parents of this kid?" Two people came forward pleading for me to not hurt their darling child. I aimed the pistol at the man, "You should have taught your child it's not polite to piss on strangers." I shot once and the man went down. The people started screaming again, and the woman dropped to his chest and cried.

"Shut up." They quieted. "Now I want one of you to call the news stations. I want to have all the major networks here to see this and hear my message." One of the men flipped out a cellphone and dialed.

Within a matter of minutes there were news vans, cops, and many others gathering around the scene. I still had the boy clutched tightly, and the gun was once again against his head. The police were telling me to drop the weapon, the boy, and surrender. "Not until I give my message. Get those cameras over here. I want all of them to hear these words."

One by one the cameras were placed in front of me. All the major networks were here. This was sure to reach everyone. "This is word from Jesus Christ himself. He spoke to me and wanted you all to hear his message. You are all guilty of forgetting the true meaning of Easter. It sickens both him and I how you get so easily swayed by advertisements of chocolate bunnies, colored marshmallows, and even more, those damnable eggs. You have all forgotten that Easter is about the resurrection of Christ. And for that, you must all pay." The crowd was silent. Some of the people were hanging their heads, most likely from shame.

I held the child up a little more and continued, "You are ruining your children and teaching them false lessons. You must all repent. You must take out the commercialism from this holiday."

One person spoke up, "But without the candy, no one cares." The man's words infuriated me. I turned and looked at him, my eyes going red. I shot the child I was holding and shot the man that spoke. The last thing I heard was the sound of other guns firing as I fell to the ground.

BEEEEEEEEEEEEEEEEEEEEEEEEEEEEEEEEP.

"We have an emergency in room 615. We need doctors quickly. The patient is flat-lining," were the words heard through the speakers. Doctors and nurses rushed to the room. The patient on the bed lay still as the doctors tried to resuscitate her, but none of their methods worked.

"At least she passed peacefully. She's even smiling," Dr. Michelson stated.

"Cause of death, heart failure. Probably from all the drugs pumped into her from Dr. Franks," one of the nurses said.

"Poor Lenora. Just when I found out that little boy with the Tabasco sauce injury was going to be fine, she dies. She seemed upset when she found out he might be hurt. I thought it would calm her down. Too bad."

Printed in Great Britain
by Amazon.co.uk, Ltd.,
Marston Gate.